JEWISH FAIRY TALES AND LEGENDS

ILLUSTRATED

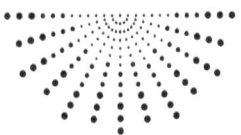

AUNT NAOMI (GERTRUDE LANDA)

ALICIA EDITIONS

When Childhood's toys have passed away,
May Books become another play.
Then may each book a blessing give
And bring you pleasure while you live.

— *RUTH LANDA.*

CONTENTS

PREFACE	1
The Palace of the Eagles	2
The Giant of the Flood	8
The Fairy Princess of Ergetz	13
The Higgledy-Piggledy Palace	28
The Red Slipper	33
The Star-Child	38
Abi Fressah's Feast	44
The Beggar King	51
The Quarrel of the Cat and Dog	55
The Water-Babe	59
Sinbad of the Talmud	63
The Outcast Prince	71
The Story of Bostanai	77
From Shepherd-Boy to King	83
The Magic Palace	86
The Sleep of One Hundred Years	91
King for Three Days	95
The Palace in the Clouds	99
The Pope's Game of Chess	105
The Slave's Fortune	111
The Paradise in the Sea	116
The Rabbi's Bogey-Man	121
The Fairy Frog	125
The Princess of the Tower	129

Part I
KING ALEXANDER'S ADVENTURES

I. THE VISION OF VICTORY	141
II. THE LAND OF DARKNESS AND THE GATE OF PARADISE	144
III--THE WONDERS OF THE WORLD	148

PREFACE

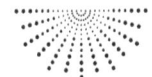

THE very cordial welcome given to my earlier volume of "Jewish Fairy Tales and Fables" has prompted me to draw further upon Rabbinic lore in the interest, chiefly, of the children. How the wise Rabbis of old took into account the necessities of the little ones, whose minds they understood so perfectly, is obvious from such legends as those dealing with boyish exploits of the great Biblical characters, Abraham, Moses, and David. These I have rewritten from the stories in the Talmud and Midrash in a manner suitable for the children of to-day.

I have ventured also beyond the confines of these two wonderful compilations. There is a wealth of delightful imagination in the legends and folk-lore of the Jews of a later period which is almost entirely unknown to children. I have drawn also on these sources for some of the stories here presented. My desire is to give boys and girls something Jewish which they may be able to regard as companion delights to the treasury of general fairy-lore and childish romance.

AUNT NAOMI.
LONDON, *March, 1919.*

THE PALACE OF THE EAGLES

East of the Land of the Rising Sun there dwelled a king who spent all his days and half his nights in pleasure. His kingdom was on the edge of the world, according to the knowledge of those times, and almost entirely surrounded by the sea. Nobody seemed to care what lay beyond the barrier of rocks that shut off the land from the rest of the world. For the matter of that, nobody appeared to trouble much about anything in that kingdom.

Most of the people followed the example of the king and led idle, careless lives, giving no thought to the future. The king regarded the task of governing his subjects as a big nuisance; he did not care to be worried with proposals concerning the welfare of the masses, and documents brought to him by his advisors for signature were never read. For aught he knew they may have referred to the school regulations of the moon, instead of the laws of trading and such like public matters.

"Don't bother me," was his usual remark. "You are my advisors and officers of state. Deal with affairs as you think best."

And off he would go to his beloved hunting which was his favorite pastime.

The land was fertile, and nobody had ever entertained an idea that bad weather might some year affect the crops and cause a scarcity of grain. They took no precautions to lay in stocks of wheat, and so when one summer there was a great lack of rain and the fields were parched, the winter that followed was marked by suffering. The kingdom was faced by famine, and the people did not like it. They did not know what to do, and when they appealed to the king, he could not help them. Indeed, he could not understand the difficulty. He passed it off very lightly.

"I am a mighty hunter," he said. "I can always kill enough beasts to provide a sufficiency of food."

But the drought had withered away the grass and the trees, and the shortage of such food had greatly reduced the number of animals. The king found the forests empty of deer and birds. Still he failed to realize the gravity of the situation and what he considered an exceedingly bright idea struck him.

"I will explore the unknown territory beyond the barrier of rocky hills," he said. "Surely there will I find a land of plenty. And, at least" he added, "it will be a pleasant adventure with good hunting."

A great expedition was therefore arranged, and the king and his hunting companions set forth to find a path over the rocks. This was not at all difficult, and on the third day, a pass was discovered among the crags and peaks that formed the summit of the barrier, and the king saw the region beyond.

It seemed a vast and beautiful land, stretching away as far as the eye could see in a forest of huge trees. Carefully, the hunters descended the other side of the rock barrier and entered the unknown land.

It seemed uninhabited. Nor was there any sign of beast or bird of any kind. No sound disturbed the stillness of the forest, no tracks were visible. As well as the hunters could make out, no foot had ever trodden the region before. Even nature seemed at rest. The trees were all old, their trunks gnarled into fantastic shapes, their leaves yellow and sere as if growth had stopped ages ago.

Altogether the march through the forest was rather eerie, and the hunters proceeded in single file, which added to the impressiveness of the strange experience. The novelty, however, made it pleasant to the king, and he kept on his way for four days.

Then the forest ended abruptly, and the explorers came to a vast open plain, a desert, through which a wide river flowed. Far beyond rose a mountain capped by rocks of regular shape. At any rate, they appeared to be rocks, but the distance was too great to enable anyone to speak with certainty.

"Water," said the vizier, "is a sign of life."

So the king decided to continue as far as the mountain. A ford was discovered in the river, and once on the other side it was possible to make out the rocks crowning the mountain. They looked too regular to be mere rocks, and on approaching nearer the king was sure that a huge building must be at the top of the mountain. When they arrived quite close, there was no doubt, about it. Either a town, or a palace, stood on the summit, and it was decided to make the ascent next day.

During the night no sound was heard, but to everybody's surprise a distinct path up the mountain was noticed in the morning. It was so overgrown with weeds and moss and straggling creepers that it was obvious it had not been used for a long time. The ascent was accordingly difficult, but half way up the first sign of life, noticed since the expedition began, made itself visible.

It was an eagle. Suddenly it flew down from the mountain top and circled above the hunters, screaming, but making no attempt to attack.

At length the summit was gained. It was a flat plateau of great expanse, almost the whole of which was covered by an enormous building of massive walls and stupendous towers.

"This is the palace of a great monarch," said the king.

But no entrance of any kind could be seen. The rest of the day was spent in wandering round, but nowhere was a door, or window, or opening visible. It was decided to make a more serious effort next morning to gain entry.

However, it seemed a greater puzzle than ever. At length, one of the most venturesome of the party discovered an eagle's nest on one of the smallest towers, and with great difficulty he secured the bird and brought it down to the king.

His majesty bade one of his wise men, Muflog, learned in bird languages, to speak to it. He did so.

In a harsh croaking voice, the eagle replied, "I am but a young bird, only seven centuries old. I know naught. On a tower higher than that on which I dwell, is the eyrie of my father. He may be able to give you information."

More he would not say. The only thing to do was to climb the higher tower and question the father eagle. This was done, and the bird answered:

"On a tower still higher dwells my father, and on yet a higher tower my grandfather, who is two thousand years old. He may know something. I know nothing."

After considerable difficulty the topmost tower was reached and the venerable bird discovered. He seemed asleep and was only awakened after much coaxing. Then he surveyed the hunters warily.

"Let me see, let me think," he muttered slowly. "I did hear, when I was a tiny eagle chick, but a few years old--that was long, long ago--that my great-grandfather had said that his great-grandfather had told him he had heard that long, long, long ago--oh, ever so much longer than that--a king lived in this palace; that he died and left it to the eagles; and that in the course of many, many, many thousands of years the door had been covered up by the dust brought by the winds."

"Where is the door?" asked Muflog.

That was a puzzle the ancient bird could not answer readily. He thought and thought and fell asleep and had to be kept being awakened until at last he remembered.

"When the sun shines in the morning," he croaked, "its first ray falls on the door."

Then, worn out with all his thinking and talking, he fell asleep again.

There was no rest for the party that night. They all watched to make certain of seeing the first ray of the rising sun strike the palace. When it did so, the spot was carefully noted. But no door could be seen. Digging was therefore begun and after many hours, an opening was found.

Through this an entrance was effected into the palace. What a wonderful and mysterious place it was, all overgrown with the weeds of centuries! Tangled masses of creepers lay everywhere over what were once trimly kept pathways, and almost completely hiding the lower buildings. In the crevices of the walls, roots had insinuated themselves, and by their growth had forced the stones apart. It was all a terrible scene of desolation. The king's men had to hack a way laboriously through the wilderness of weeds with their swords to the central building, and when they did so they came to a door on which was an inscription cut deep into the wood. The language was unknown to all but Muflog, who deciphered it as follows:

> "We, the Dwellers in this Palace, lived for many years in Comfort and Luxury. Then Hunger came. We had made no preparation. We had amassed jewels in abundance but not Corn. We ground Pearls and Rubies to fine flour, but could make no Bread. Wherefore we die, bequeathing this Palace to the eagles who will devour our bodies and build their eyries on our towers."

A dread silence fell on the whole party when Muflog read these strange words, and the king turned pale. This warning from the dead past was making the adventure far from enjoyable. Some of the party suggested the immediate abandonment of the expedition and the prompt return home. They feared hidden dangers now. But the king remained resolute.

"I must investigate this to the end," he said in a firm voice. "Those who are seized by fear may return. I will go on, if needs be, alone."

Encouraged by these words, the hunters decided to remain with the king. One of them began to batter at the door, but the king was anxious to preserve the inscription, and after more cutting away of weeds, the key was seen to be sticking in the keyhole. Unlocking the door, however, was no light task, for ages of rust had accumulated. When finally this was accomplished the door creaked heavily on its hinges and a musty smell came from the dank corridor that was revealed.

The explorers walked ankle-deep in dust through a maze of rooms until they came to a big central hall of statues. So artistically fashioned were they that they seemed lifelike in their attitudes, and for a moment all held their breath. This hall was dustless, and Muflog pointed out that it was an airtight chamber. Evidently it had been specifically devised to preserve the statues.

"These must be the effigies of kings," said his majesty, and on reading the inscriptions, Muflog said that was so.

At the far end of the hall, on a pedestal higher than the others, was a statue bigger than the rest. In addition to the name there was an inscription on the pedestal. Muflog read it amid an awed stillness:

"I am the last of the kings--yea, the last of men, and with my own hands have completed this work. I ruled over a thousand cities, rode on a thousand horses, and received the homage of a thousand vassal princes; but when Famine came I was powerless. Ye who may read this, take heed of the fate that has overwhelmed this land. Take but one word of counsel from the last of the mortals; prepare thy meal while the daylight lasts * * *"

The words broke off: the rest was undecipherable.

"Enough," cried the king, and his voice was not steady. "This has indeed been good hunting. I have learned, in my folly and pursuit of pleasure, what I had failed to see for myself. Let us return and act upon the counsel of this king who has met the end that will surely be our own should we forget his warning."

Looking out across the plain they had traversed, his majesty seemed to see a vision of prosperous cities and smiling fertile fields. In imagination, he saw caravans laden with merchandise journeying across the intervening spaces. Then, as darker thoughts followed, a cloud appeared to settle over the whole land. The cities crumbled and disappeared, the eagles swooped down and took possession of that which man had failed to appreciate and hold; and after the eagles the dust of the ages settled slowly, piling itself up year by year until everything was covered and only the desert was visible.

Scarcely a word was spoken as the king and his hunters made their way back to the land East of the Rising Sun. In all, they had been away forty days when they re-crossed the barrier of rocks. They were joyously welcomed.

"What have you brought," asked the populace. "In a little while we shall be starving."

"Ye shall not starve," said the king. "I have brought wisdom from the Palace of the Eagles. From the fate and sufferings of others I have learned a lesson--my duty."

At once he set to work to organize the proper distribution of the food supply and the cultivation of the land. He wasted no more time on foolish pleasures, and in due course the land East of the Rising Sun enjoyed happiness and prosperity and even established fruitful colonies in the plain overlooked by the Palace of the Eagles.

THE GIANT OF THE FLOOD

*J*ust before the world was drowned all the animals gathered in front of the Ark and Father Noah carefully inspected them.

"All ye that lie down shall enter and be saved from the deluge that is about to destroy the world," he said. "Ye that stand cannot enter."

Then the various creatures began to march forward into the Ark. Father Noah watched them closely. He seemed troubled.

"I wonder," he said to himself, "how I shall obtain a unicorn, and how I shall get it into the Ark."

"I can bring thee a unicorn, Father Noah," he heard in a voice of thunder, and turning round he saw the giant, Og. "But thou must agree to save me, too, from the flood."

"Begone," cried Noah. "Thou art a demon, not a human being. I can have no dealings with thee."

"Pity me," whined the giant. "See how my figure is shrinking. Once I was so tall that I could drink water from the clouds and toast fish at the sun. I fear not that I shall be drowned, but that all the food will be destroyed and that I shall perish of hunger."

Noah, however, only smiled; but he grew serious again when Og brought a unicorn. It was as big as a mountain, although the giant said it was the smallest he could find. It lay down in front of the Ark and Noah saw by that action that he must save it. For some time he was puzzled what to do, but at last a bright idea struck him. He attached the huge beast to the Ark by a rope fastened to its horn so that it could swim alongside and be fed.

Og seated himself on a mountain near at hand and watched the rain pouring down. Faster and faster it fell in torrents until the rivers overflowed and the waters began to rise rapidly on the land and sweep all things away. Father Noah stood gloomily before the door of the Ark until the water reached his neck. Then it swept him inside. The door closed with a bang, and the Ark rose gallantly on the flood and began to move along. The unicorn swam alongside, and as it passed Og, the giant jumped on to its back.

"See, Father Noah," he cried, with a huge chuckle, "you will have to save me after all. I will snatch all the food you put through the window for the unicorn."

Noah saw that it was useless to argue with Og, who might, indeed, sink the Ark with his tremendous strength.

"I will make a bargain with thee," he shouted from a window. "I will feed thee, but thou must promise to be a servant to my descendants."

Og was very hungry, so he accepted the conditions and devoured his first breakfast.

The rain continued to fall in great big sheets that shut out the light of day. Inside the Ark, however, all was bright and cheerful, for Noah had collected the most precious of the stones of the earth and had used them for the windows. Their radiance illumined the whole of the three stories in the Ark. Some of the animals were troublesome and Noah got no sleep at all. The lion had a bad attack of fever. In a corner a bird slept the whole of the time. This was the phoenix.

"Wake up," said Noah, one day. "It is feeding time."

"Thank you," returned the bird. "I saw thou wert busy, Father Noah, so I would not trouble thee."

"Thou art a good bird," said Noah, much touched, "therefore thou shalt never die."

One day the rain ceased, the clouds rolled away and the sun shone brilliantly again. How strange the world looked! It was like a vast ocean. Nothing but water could be seen anywhere, and only one or two of the highest mountain tops peeped above the flood. All the world was drowned, and Noah gazed on the desolate scene from one of the windows with tears in his eyes. Og, riding gaily on the unicorn behind the Ark, was quite happy.

"Ha, ha!" he laughed gleefully. "I shall be able to eat and drink just as much as I like now and shall never be troubled by those tiny little creatures, the mortals."

"Be not so sure," said Noah. "Those tiny mortals shall be thy masters and shall outlive thee and the whole race of giants and demons."

The giant did not relish this prospect. He knew that whatever Noah prophesied would come true, and he was so sad that he ate no food for two days and began to grow smaller and thinner. He became more and more unhappy as day by day the water subsided and the mountains began to appear. At last the Ark rested on Mount Ararat, and Og's long ride came to an end.

"I will soon leave thee, Father Noah," he said. "I shall wander round the world to see what is left of it."

"Thou canst not go until I permit thee," said Noah. "Hast thou forgotten our compact so soon? Thou must be my servant. I have work for thee."

Giants are not fond of work, and Og, who was the father of all the giants, was particularly lazy. He cared only to eat and sleep, but he knew he was in Noah's power, and he shed bitter tears when he saw the land appear again.

"Stop," commanded Noah. "Dost thou wish to drown the world once more with thy big tears?"

So Og sat on a mountain and rocked from side to side, weeping silently to himself. He watched the animals leave the Ark and had to do all the hard work when Noah's children built houses. Daily he complained that he was shrinking to the size of the mortals, for Noah said there was not too much food.

One day Noah said to him, "Come with me, Og. I am going around the world. I am commanded to plant fruit and flowers to make the earth beautiful. I need thy help."

For many days they wandered all over the earth, and Og was compelled to carry the heavy bag of seeds. The last thing Noah planted was the grape vine.

"What is this--food, or drink?" asked Og.

"Both," replied Noah. "It can be eaten, or its juice made into wine," and as he planted it, he blessed the grape. "Be thou," he said, "a plant pleasing to the eye, bear fruit that will be food for the hungry and a health-giving drink to the thirsty and sick."

Og grunted.

"I will offer up sacrifice to this wonderful fruit," he said. "May I not do so now that our labors are over?"

Noah agreed, and the giant brought a sheep, a lion, a pig and a monkey. First, he slaughtered the sheep, then the lion.

"When a man shall taste but a few drops of the wine," he said, "he shall be as harmless as a sheep. When he takes a little more he shall be as strong as a lion."

Then Og began to dance around the plant, and he killed the pig and the monkey. Noah was very much surprised.

"I am giving thy descendants two extra blessings," said Og, chuckling.

He rolled over and over on the ground in great glee and then said:

"When a man shall drink too much of the juice of the wine, then shall he become a beast like the pig, and if then he still continues to drink, he shall behave foolishly like a monkey."

And that is why, unto this day, too much wine makes a man silly.

Og himself often drank too much, and many years afterward, when he was a servant to the patriarch Abraham, the latter scolded him until he became so frightened that he dropped a tooth. Abraham made an ivory chair for himself from this tooth. Afterwards Og became King of Bashan, but he forgot his compact with Noah and instead of helping the Israelites to obtain Canaan he opposed them.

"I will kill them all with one blow," he declared.

Exerting all his enormous strength he uprooted a mountain, and raising it high above his head he prepared to drop it on the camp of the Israelites and crush it.

But a wonderful thing happened. The mountain was full of grasshoppers and ants who had bored millions of tiny holes in it. When King Og raised the great mass it crumbled in his hands and fell over his head and round his neck like a collar. He tried to pull it off, but his teeth became entangled in the mass. As he danced about in rage and pain, Moses, the leader of the Israelites, approached him.

Moses was a tiny man compared with Og. He was only ten ells high, and he carried with him a sword of the same length. With a mighty effort he jumped ten ells into the air, and raising the sword, he managed to strike the giant on the ankle and wound him mortally.

Thus, after many years, did the terrible giant of the flood perish for breaking his word to Father Noah.

THE FAIRY PRINCESS OF ERGETZ

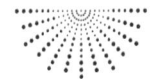

I

*I*n a great and beautiful city that stood by the sea, an old man lay dying. Mar Shalmon was his name, and he was the richest man in the land. Propped up with pillows on a richly decorated bed in a luxurious chamber, he gazed, with tears in his eyes, through the open window at the setting sun. Like a ball of fire it sank lower and lower until it almost seemed to rest on the tranquil waters beyond the harbor. Suddenly, Mar Shalmon roused himself.

"Where is my son, Bar Shalmon?" he asked in a feeble voice, and his hand crept tremblingly along the silken coverlet of the bed as if in search of something.

"I am here, my father," replied his son who was standing by the side of his bed. His eyes were moist with tears, but his voice was steady.

"My son," said the old man, slowly, and with some difficulty, "I am about to leave this world.

My soul will take flight from this frail body when the sun has sunk behind the horizon. I have lived long and have amassed great wealth which will soon be thine. Use it well, as I have taught thee, for thou, my son, art a man of learning, as befits our noble Jewish faith. One thing I must ask thee to promise me."

"I will, my father," returned Bar Shalmon, sobbing.

"Nay, weep not, my son," said the old man. "My day is ended; my life has not been ill-spent. I would spare thee the pain that was mine in my early days, when, as a merchant, I garnered my fortune. The sea out there that will soon swallow up the sun is calm now. But beware of it, my son, for it is treacherous. Promise me--nay, swear unto me--that never wilt thou cross it to foreign lands."

Bar Shalmon placed his hands on those of his father.

"Solemnly I swear," he said, in a broken voice, "to do thy wish--never to journey on the sea, but to remain here in this, my native land. 'Tis a vow before thee, my father."

"'Tis an oath before heaven," said the old man. "Guard it, keep it, and heaven will bless thee. Remember! See, the sun is sinking."

Mar Shalmon fell back upon his pillows and spoke no more. Bar Shalmon stood gazing out of the window until the sun had disappeared, and then, silently sobbing, he left the chamber of death.

The whole city wept when the sad news was made known, for Mar Shalmon was a man of great charity, and almost all the inhabitants followed the remains to the grave. Then Bar Shalmon, his son, took his father's place of honor in the city, and in him, too, the poor and needy found a friend whose purse was ever open and whose counsel was ever wisdom.

Thus years passed away.

One day there arrived in the harbor of the city a strange ship from a distant land. Its captain spoke a tongue unknown, and Bar Shalmon, being a man of profound knowledge, was sent for. He alone in the city could under-stand the language of the captain. To his astonishment, he learned that the cargo of the vessel was for Mar Shalmon, his father.

"I am the son of Mar Shalmon," he said. "My father is dead, and all his possessions he left to me."

"Then, verily, art thou the most fortunate mortal, and the richest, on earth," answered the captain. "My good ship is filled with a vast store of jewels, precious stones and other treasures. And know you, O most favored son of Mar Shalmon, this cargo is but a small portion of the wealth that is thine in a land across the sea."

"'Tis strange," said Bar Shalmon, in surprise; "my father said nought of this to me. I knew that in his younger days he had traded with distant lands, but nothing did he ever say of possessions there. And, moreover, he warned me never to leave this shore."

The captain looked perplexed.

"I understand it not," he said. "I am but performing my father's bidding. He was thy father's servant, and long years did he wait for Mar

Shalmon's return to claim his riches. On his death-bed he bade me vow that I would seek his master, or his son, and this have I done."

He produced documents, and there could be no doubt that the vast wealth mentioned in them belonged now to Bar Shalmon.

"Thou art now my master," said the captain, "and must return with me to the land across the sea to claim thine inheritance. In another year it will be too late, for by the laws of the country it will be forfeit."

"I cannot return with thee," said Bar Shalmon. "I have a vow before heaven never to voyage on the sea."

The captain laughed.

"In very truth, I understand thee not, as my father understood not thine," he replied. "My father was wont to say that Mar Shalmon was strange and peradventure not possessed of all his senses to neglect his store of wealth and treasure."

With an angry gesture Bar Shalmon stopped the captain, but he was sorely troubled. He re-called now that his father had often spoken mysteriously of foreign lands, and he wondered, indeed, whether Mar Shalmon could have been in his proper senses not to have breathed a word of his riches abroad. For days he discussed the matter with the captain, who at last persuaded him to make the journey.

"Fear not thy vow," said the captain. "Thy worthy father must, of a truth, have been bereft of reason in failing to tell thee of his full estate, and an oath to a man of mind unsound is not binding. That is the law in our land."

"So it is here," returned Bar Shalmon, and with this remark his last scruple vanished.

He bade a tender farewell to his wife, his child, and his friends, and set sail on the strange ship to the land beyond the sea.

For three days all went well, but on the fourth the ship was becalmed and the sails flapped lazily against the masts. The sailors had nothing to do but lie on deck and wait for a breeze, and Bar Shalmon took advantage of the occasion to treat them to a feast.

Suddenly, in the midst of the feasting, they felt the ship begin to move. There was no wind, but the vessel sped along very swiftly. The captain himself rushed to the helm. To his alarm he found the vessel beyond control.

"The ship is bewitched," he exclaimed. "There is no wind, and no current, and yet we are being borne along as if driven before a storm. We shall be lost."

Panic seized the sailors, and Bar Shalmon was unable to pacify them.

"Someone on board has brought us ill-luck," said the boatswain, looking pointedly at Bar Shalmon; "we shall have to heave him overboard."

His comrades assented and rushed toward Bar Shalmon.

Just at that moment, however, the look-out in the bow cried excitedly, "Land ahead!" The ship still refused to answer the helm and grounded on a sandbank. She shivered from stem to stern but did not break up. No rocks were visible, only a desolate tract of desert land was to be seen, with here and there a solitary tree.

"We seem to have sustained no damage," said the captain, when he had recovered from his first astonishment, "but how we are going to get afloat again I do not know. This land is quite strange to me."

He could not find it marked on any of his charts or maps, and the sailors stood looking gloomily at the mysterious shore.

"Had we not better explore the land?" said Bar Shalmon.

"No, no," exclaimed the boatswain, excitedly. "See, no breakers strike on the shore. This is not a human land. This is a domain of demons. We are lost unless we cast overboard the one who has brought on us this ill-luck."

Said Bar Shalmon, "I will land, and I will give fifty silver crowns to all who land with me."

Not one of the sailors moved, however, even when he offered fifty golden crowns, and at last Bar Shalmon said he would land alone, although the captain strongly urged him not to do so.

Bar Shalmon sprang lightly to the shore, and as he did so the ship shook violently.

"What did I tell you?" shouted the boat-swain. "Bar Shalmon is the one who has brought us this misfortune. Now we shall re-float the ship."

But it still remained firmly fixed on the sand. Bar Shalmon walked towards a tree and climbed it. In a few moments he returned, holding a twig in his hand.

"The land stretches away for miles just as you see it here," he called to the captain. "There is no sign of man or habitation."

He prepared to board the vessel again, but the sailors would not allow him. The boatswain stood in the bow and threatened him with a sword. Bar Shalmon raised the twig to ward off the blow and struck the ship which shivered from stem to stern again.

"Is not this proof that the vessel is bewitched?" cried the sailors, and when the captain sternly bade them remember that Bar Shalmon was their master, they threatened him too.

Bar Shalmon, amused at the fears of the men, again struck the vessel with the twig. Once more it trembled. A third time he raised the twig.

"If the ship is bewitched," he said, "something will happen after the third blow."

"Swish" sounded the branch through the air, and the third blow fell on the vessel's bow. Something did happen. The ship almost leaped from the sand, and before Bar Shalmon could realize what had happened it was speeding swiftly away.

"Come back, come back," he screamed, and he could see the captain struggling with the helm. But the vessel refused to answer, and Bar Shalmon saw it grow smaller and smaller and finally disappear. He was alone on an uninhabited desert land.

"What a wretched plight for the richest man in the world," he said to himself, and the next moment he realized that he was in danger indeed.

A terrible roar made him look around. To his horror he saw a lion making toward him. As quick as a flash Bar Shalmon ran to the tree and hastily scrambled into the branches. The lion dashed itself furiously against the trunk of the tree, but, for the present, Bar Shalmon was safe. Night, however, was coming on, and the lion squatted at the foot of the tree, evidently intending to wait for him. All night the lion remained, roaring at intervals, and Bar Shalmon clung to one of the upper branches afraid to sleep lest he should fall off and be devoured. When morning broke, a new danger threatened him. A huge eagle flew round the tree and darted at him with its cruel beak. Then the great bird settled on the thickest branch, and Bar Shalmon moved stealthily forward with a knife which he drew from his belt. He crept behind the bird, but as he approached it spread its big wings, and Bar Shalmon, to prevent himself being swept from the tree, dropped the knife and clutched at the bird's feathers. Immediately, to his dismay, the bird rose from the tree. Bar Shalmon clung to its back with all his might.

Higher and higher soared the eagle until the trees below looked like mere dots on the land. Swiftly flew the eagle over miles and miles of desert until Bar Shalmon began to feel giddy. He was faint with hunger and feared that he would not be able to retain his hold. All day the bird flew without resting, across island and sea. No houses, no ships, no human beings could be seen. Toward night, however, Bar Shalmon, to his great joy, beheld the lights of a city surrounded by trees, and as the eagle came near, he made a bold dive to the earth. Headlong he plunged downward. He seemed to be hours in falling. At last he struck a tree. The branches broke beneath the weight and force of his falling body, and he continued to plunge downward. The branches tore his clothes to shreds and bruised his body, but they broke his terrible fall, and when at last he reached the ground he was not much hurt.

II

Bar Shalmon found himself on the outskirts of the city, and cautiously he crept forward. To his intense relief, he saw that the first building was a synagogue. The door, however, was locked. Weary, sore, and weak with long fasting, Bar Shalmon sank down on the steps and sobbed like a child.

Something touched him on the arm. He looked up. By the light of the moon he saw a boy standing before him. Such a queer boy he was, too. He had cloven feet, and his coat, if it was a coat, seemed to be made in the shape of wings.

"*Ivri Onochi*," said Bar Shalmon, "I am a Hebrew."

"So am I," said the boy. "Follow me."

He walked in front with a strange hobble, and when they reached a house at the back of the synagogue, he leaped from the ground, spreading his coat wings as he did so, to a window about twenty feet from the ground. The next moment a door opened, and Bar Shalmon, to his surprise, saw that the boy had jumped straight through the window down to the door which he had unfastened from the inside. The boy motioned him to enter a room. He did so. An aged man, who he saw was a rabbi, rose to greet him.

"Peace be with you," said the rabbi, and pointed to a seat. He clapped his hand and immediately a table with food appeared before Bar Shalmon. The latter was far too hungry to ask any questions just then, and the rabbi was silent, too, while he ate. When he had finished, the rabbi clapped his hands and the table vanished.

"Now tell me your story," said the rabbi. Bar Shalmon did so.

"Alas! I am an unhappy man," he concluded. "I have been punished for breaking my vow. Help me to return to my home. I will reward thee well, and will atone for my sin."

"Thy story is indeed sad," said the rabbi, gravely, "but thou knowest not the full extent of thy unfortunate plight. Art thou aware what land it is into which thou hast been cast?"

"No," said Bar Shalmon, becoming afraid again.

"Know then," said the rabbi, "thou art not in a land of human beings. Thou hast fallen into Ergetz, the land of demons, of djinns, and of fairies."

"But art thou not a Jew?" asked Bar Shalmon, in astonishment.

"Truly," replied the rabbi. "Even in this realm we have all manner of religions just as you mortals have."

"What will happen to me?" asked Bar Shalmon, in a whisper.

"I know not," replied the rabbi. "Few mortals come here, and mostly, I fear they are put to death. The demons love them not."

"Woe, woe is me," cried Bar Shalmon, "I am undone."

"Weep not," said the rabbi. "I, as a Jew, love not death by violence and torture, and will endeavor to save thee."

"I thank thee," cried Bar Shalmon.

"Let thy thanks wait," said the rabbi, kindly. "There is human blood in my veins. My great-grandfather was a mortal who fell into this land and was not put to death. Being of mortal descent, I have been made rabbi. Perhaps thou wilt find favor here and be permitted to live and settle in this land."

"But I desire to return home," said Bar Shalmon.

The rabbi shook his head.

"Thou must sleep now," he said.

He passed his hands over Bar Shalmon's eyes and he fell into a profound slumber. When he awoke it was daylight, and the boy stood by his couch. He made a sign to Bar Shalmon to follow, and through an underground passage he conducted him into the synagogue and placed him near the rabbi.

"Thy presence has become known," whispered the rabbi, and even as he spoke a great noise was heard. It was like the wild chattering of many high-pitched voices. Through all the windows and the doors a strange crowd poured into the synagogue. There were demons of all shapes and sizes. Some had big bodies with tiny heads, others huge heads and quaint little bodies. Some had great staring eyes, others had long wide mouths, and many had only one leg each. They surrounded Bar Shalmon with threatening gestures and noises. The rabbi ascended the pulpit.

"Silence!" he commanded, and immediately the noise ceased. "Ye who thirst for mortal blood, desecrate not this holy building wherein I am master. What ye have to say must wait until after the morning service."

Silently and patiently they waited, sitting in all manner of queer places. Some of them perched on the backs of the seats, a few clung like great big flies to the pillars, others sat on the window-sills, and several of the tiniest hung from the rafters in the ceiling. As soon as the service was over, the clamor broke out anew.

"Give to us the perjurer," screamed the demons. "He is not fit to live."

With some difficulty, the rabbi stilled the tumult, and said:

"Listen unto me, ye demons and sprites of the land of Ergetz. This man has fallen into my hands, and I am responsible for him. Our king, Ashmedai, must know of his arrival. We must not condemn a man unheard. Let us petition the king to grant him a fair trial."

After some demur, the demons agreed to this proposal, and they trooped out of the synagogue in the same peculiar manner in which they came.

Each was compelled to leave by the same door or window at which he entered.

Bar Shalmon was carried off to the palace of King Ashmedai, preceded and followed by a noisy crowd of demons and fairies. There seemed to be millions of them, all clattering and pointing at him. They hobbled and hopped over the ground, jumped into the air, sprang from housetop to housetop, made sudden appearances from holes in the ground and vanished through solid walls.

The palace was a vast building of white marble that seemed as delicate as lace work. It stood in a magnificent square where many beautiful fountains spouted jets of crystal water. King Ashmedai came forth on the balcony, and at his appearance all the demons and fairies became silent and went down on their knees.

"What will ye with me?" he cried, in a voice of thunder, and the rabbi approached and bowed before his majesty.

"A mortal, a Jew, has fallen into my hands," he said, "and thy subjects crave for his blood. He is a perjurer, they say. Gracious majesty, I would petition for a trial."

"What manner of mortal is he?" asked Ashmedai.

Bar Shalmon stepped forward.

"Jump up here so I may see thee," commanded the king.

"Jump, jump," cried the crowd.

"I cannot," said Bar Shalmon, as he looked up at the balcony thirty feet above the ground. "Try," said the rabbi.

Bar Shalmon did try, and found, the moment he lifted his feet from the ground, that he was standing on the balcony.

"Neatly done," said the king. "I see thou art quick at learning."

"So my teachers always said," replied Bar Shalmon.

"A proper answer," said the king. "Thou art, then, a scholar."

"In my own land," returned Bar Shalmon, "men said I was great among the learned."

"So," said the king. "And canst thou impart the wisdom of man and of the human world to others?"

"I can," said Bar Shalmon.

"We shall see," said the king. "I have a son with a desire for such knowledge. If thou canst make him acquainted with thy store of learning, thy life shall be spared. The petition for a trial is granted."

The king waved his scepter and two slaves seized Bar Shalmon by the arms. He felt himself lifted from the balcony and carried swiftly through the air. Across the vast square the slaves flew with him, and when over the largest of the fountains they loosened their hold. Bar Shalmon thought he would fall into the fountain, but to his amazement he found himself standing on the roof of a building. By his side was the rabbi.

"Where are we?" asked Bar Shalmon. "I feel bewildered."

"We are at the Court of Justice, one hundred miles from the palace," replied the rabbi.

A door appeared before them. They stepped through, and found themselves in a beautiful hall. Three judges in red robes and purple wigs were seated on a platform, and an immense crowd filled the galleries in the same queer way as in the synagogue. Bar Shalmon was placed on a small platform in front of the judges. A tiny sprite, only about six inches high, stood on another small platform at his right hand and commenced to read from a scroll that seemed to have no ending. He read the whole account of Bar Shalmon's life. Not one little event was missing.

"The charge against Bar Shalmon, the mortal," the sprite concluded, "is that he has violated the solemn oath sworn at his father's death-bed."

Then the rabbi pleaded for him and declared that the oath was not binding because Bar Shalmon's father had not informed him of his treasures abroad and could not therefore have been in his right senses. Further, he added, Bar Shalmon was a scholar and the king desired him to teach his wisdom to the crown prince.

The chief justice rose to pronounce sentence.

"Bar Shalmon," he said, "rightly thou shouldst die for thy broken oath.

It is a grievous sin. But there is the doubt that thy father may not have been in his right mind. Therefore, thy life shall be spared."

Bar Shalmon expressed his thanks.

"When may I return to my home?" he asked. "Never," replied the chief justice.

Bar Shalmon left the court, feeling very downhearted. He was safe now. The demons dared not molest him, but he longed to return to his home.

"How am I to get back to the palace?" he asked the rabbi. "Perhaps after I have imparted my learning to the crown prince, the king will allow me to return to my native land."

"That I cannot say. Come, fly with me," said the rabbi.

"Fly!"

"Yes; see thou hast wings."

Bar Shalmon noticed that he was now wearing a garment just like all the demons. When he spread his arms, he found he could fly, and he sailed swiftly through the air to the palace. With these wings, he thought, he would be able to fly home.

"Think not that," said the rabbi, who seemed to be able to read his thoughts, "for thy wings are useless beyond this land."

Bar Shalmon found that it would be best for him to carry out his instructions for the present, and he set himself diligently to teach the crown prince. The prince was an apt pupil, and the two became great friends. King Ashmedai was delighted and made Bar Shalmon one of his favorites.

One day the king said to him: "I am about to leave the city for a while to undertake a campaign against a rebellious tribe of demons thousands of miles away. I must take the crown prince with me. I leave thee in charge of the palace."

The king gave him a huge bunch of keys.

"These," he said, "will admit into all but one of the thousand rooms in the palace. For that one there is no key, and thou must not enter it. Beware."

For several days Bar Shalmon amused himself by examining the hundreds of rooms in the vast palace until one day he came to the door for which he had no key. He forgot the king's warning and his promise to obey.

"Open this door for me," he said to his attendants, but they replied that they could not.

"You must," he said angrily, "burst it open."

"We do not know how to burst open a door," they said. "We are not mortal. If we were permitted to enter the room we should just walk through the walls."

Bar Shalmon could not do this, so he put his shoulder to the door and it yielded quite easily.

A strange sight met his gaze. A beautiful woman, the most beautiful he had ever seen, was seated on a throne of gold, surrounded by fairy attendants who vanished the moment he entered.

"Who art thou?" asked Bar Shalmon, in great astonishment.

"The daughter of the king," replied the princess, "and thy future wife."

"Indeed! How know you that?" he asked.

"Thou hast broken thy promise to my father, the king, not to enter this room," she replied. "Therefore, thou must die, unless--"

"Tell me quickly," interrupted Bar Shalmon, turning pale, "how my life can be saved."

"Thou must ask my father for my hand," replied the princess. "Only by becoming my husband canst thou be saved."

"But I have a wife and child in my native land," said Bar Shalmon, sorely troubled.

"Thou hast now forfeited thy hopes of return," said the princess, slowly. "Once more hast thou broken a promise. It seems to come easy to thee now."

Bar Shalmon had no wish to die, and he waited, in fear and trembling for the king's re-turn. Immediately he heard of King Ashmedai's approach, he hastened to meet him and flung himself on the ground at his majesty's feet.

"O King," he cried, "I have seen thy daughter, the princess, and I desire to make her my wife."

"I cannot refuse," returned the king. "Such is our law--that he who first sees the princess must become her husband, or die. But, have a care, Bar Shalmon. Thou must swear to love and be faithful ever."

"I swear," said Bar Shalmon.

The wedding took place with much ceremony. The princess was attended by a thousand fairy bridesmaids, and the whole city was brilliantly decorated and illuminated until Bar Shalmon was almost blinded by the dazzling spectacle.

The rabbi performed the marriage ceremony, and Bar Shalmon had to swear an oath by word of mouth and in writing that he loved the princess and would never desert her. He was given a beautiful palace full of jewels as a dowry, and the wedding festivities lasted six months. All the fairies and demons invited them in turn; they had to attend banquets and parties and dances in grottoes and caves and in the depths of the fairy fountains in the square. Never before in Ergetz had there been such elaborate rejoicings.

III

Some years rolled by and still Bar Shalmon thought of his native land. One day the princess found him weeping quietly.

"Why art thou sad, husband mine?" she asked. "Dost thou no longer love me, and am I not beautiful now?"

"No, it is not that," he said, but for a long time he refused to say more. At last he confessed that he had an intense longing to see his home again.

"But thou art bound to me by an oath," said the princess.

"I know," replied Bar Shalmon, "and I shall not break it. Permit me to visit my home for a brief while, and I will return and prove myself more devoted to thee than ever."

On these conditions, the princess agreed that he should take leave for a whole year. A big, black demon flew swiftly with him to his native city.

No sooner had Bar Shalmon placed his feet on the ground than he determined not to return to the land of Ergetz.

"Tell thy royal mistress," he said to the demon, "that I shall never return to her."

He tore his clothes to make himself look poor, but his wife was overjoyed to see him. She had mourned him as dead. He did not tell of his adventures, but merely said he had been ship-wrecked and had worked his way back as a poor sailor. He was delighted to be among human beings again, to hear his own language and to see solid buildings that did not appear and disappear just when they pleased, and as the days passed he began to think his adventures in fairyland were but a dream.

Meanwhile, the princess waited patiently until the year was ended.

Then she sent the big, black demon to bring Bar Shalmon back.

Bar Shalmon met the messenger one night when walking alone in his garden.

"I have come to take thee back," said the demon.

Bar Shalmon was startled. He had forgotten that the year was up. He felt that he was lost, but as the demon did not seize him by force, he saw that there was a possibility of escape.

"Return and tell thy mistress I refuse," he said.

"I will take thee by force," said the demon. "Thou canst not," Bar Shalmon said, "for I am the son-in-law of the king."

The demon was helpless and returned to Ergetz alone.

King Ashmedai was very angry, but the princess counseled patience.

"I will devise means to bring my husband back," she said. "I will send other messengers."

Thus it was that Bar Shalmon found a troupe of beautiful fairies in the garden the next evening.

They tried their utmost to induce him to return with them, but he would not listen. Every day different messengers came--big, ugly demons who threatened, pretty fairies who tried to coax him, and troublesome sprites and goblins who only annoyed him. Bar Shalmon could not move without encountering messengers from the princess in all manner of queer places. Nobody else could see them, and often he was heard talking to invisible people. His friends began to regard him as strange in his behavior.

King Ashmedai grew angrier every day, and he threatened to go for Bar Shalmon himself.

"Nay, I will go," said the princess; "it will be impossible for my husband to resist me."

She selected a large number of attendants, and the swift flight of the princess and her retinue through the air caused a violent storm to rage over the lands they crossed. Like a thick black cloud they swooped down on the land where Bar Shalmon dwelt, and their weird cries seemed like the wild shrieking of a mighty hurricane. Down they swept in a tremendous storm such as the city had never known. Then, as quickly as it came, the storm ceased, and the people who had fled into their houses, ventured forth again.

The little son of Bar Shalmon went out into the garden, but quickly rushed back into the house.

"Father, come forth and see," he cried. "The garden is full of strange creatures brought by the storm. All manner of creeping, crawling things have invaded the garden--lizards, toads, and myriads of insects. The trees, the shrubs, the paths are covered, and some shine in the twilight like tiny lanterns."

Bar Shalmon went out into the garden, but he did not see toads and lizards. What he beheld was a vast array of demons and goblins and sprites, and in a rose-bush the princess, his wife, shining like a star, surrounded by her attendant fairies. She stretched forth her arms to him.

"Husband mine," she pleaded, "I have come to implore thee to return to the land of Ergetz with me. Sadly have I missed thee; long have I waited for thy coming, and difficult has it been to appease my father's anger. Come, husband mine, return with me; a great welcome awaits thee."

"I will not return," said Bar Shalmon.

"Kill him, kill him," shrieked the demons, and they surrounded him, gesticulating fiercely. "Nay, harm him not," commanded the princess.

"Think well, Bar Shalmon, ere you answer again. The sun has set and night is upon us. Think well, until sunrise. Come to me, return, and all shall be well. Refuse, and thou shalt be dealt with as thou hast merited. Think well before the sunrise."

"And what will happen at sunrise, if I refuse?" asked Bar Shalmon.

"Thou shalt see," returned the princess. "Bethink thee well, and remember, I await thee here until the sunrise."

"I have answered; I defy thee," said Bar Shalmon, and he went indoors.

Night passed with strange, mournful music in the garden, and the sun rose in its glory and spread its golden beams over the city. And with the coming of the light, more strange sounds woke the people of the city. A wondrous sight met their gaze in the market place. It was filled with hundreds upon hundreds of the queerest creatures they had ever seen, goblins and brownies, demons and fairies. Dainty little elves ran about the square to the delight of the children, and quaint sprites clambered up the lampposts and squatted on the gables of the council house. On the steps of that building was a glittering array of fairies and attendant genii, and in their midst stood the princess, a dazzling vision, radiant as the dawn.

The mayor of the city knew not what to do. He put on his chain of office and made a long speech of welcome to the princess.

"Thank you for your cordial welcome," said the princess, in reply, "and you the mayor,. and ye the good people of this city of mortals, hearken unto me. I am the princess of the Fairyland of Ergetz where my father, Ashmedai, rules as king. There is one among ye who is my husband."

"Who is he?" the crowd asked in astonishment.

"Bar Shalmon is his name," replied the princess, "and to him am I bound by vows that may not be broken."

"'Tis false," cried Bar Shalmon from the crowd.

"'Tis true. Behold our son," answered the princess, and there stepped forward a dainty elfin boy whose face was the image of Bar Shalmon.

"I ask of you mortals of the city," the princess continued, "but one thing, justice--that same justice which we in the land of Ergetz did give unto Bar Shalmon when, after breaking his oath unto his father, he set sail for a foreign land and was delivered into our hands. We spared his life; we granted his petition for a new trial. I but ask that ye should grant me the same petition. Hear me in your Court of Justice."

"Thy request is but reasonable, princess," said the mayor. "It shall not be said that strangers here are refused justice. Bar Shalmon, follow me."

He led the way into the Chamber of Justice, and the magistrates of the city heard all that the princess and her witnesses, among whom was the rabbi, and also all that Bar Shalmon, had to say.

"'Tis plain," said the mayor, delivering judgment, "that her royal highness, the princess of the Fairyland of Ergetz, has spoken that which is true. But Bar Shalmon has in this city wife and child to whom he is bound by ties that may not be broken. Bar Shalmon must divorce the princess and return unto her the dowry received by him on their marriage."

"If such be your law, I am content," said the princess.

"What sayest thou, Bar Shalmon?" asked the mayor.

"Oh! I'm content," he answered gruffly. "I agree to anything that will rid me of the demon princess."

The princess flushed crimson with shame and rage at these cruel words.

"These words I have not deserved," she exclaimed, proudly. "I have loved thee, and have been faithful unto thee, Bar Shalmon. I accept the decree of your laws and shall return to the land of Ergetz a widow. I ask not for your pity. I ask but for that which is my right, one last kiss."

"Very well," said Bar Shalmon, still more gruffly, "anything to have done with thee."

The princess stepped proudly forward to him and kissed him on the lips.

Bar Shalmon turned deadly pale and would have fallen had not his friends caught him.

"Take thy punishment for all thy sins," cried the princess, haughtily, "for thy broken vows and thy false promises--thy perjury to thy God, to thy father, to my father and to me."

As she spoke Bar Shalmon fell dead at her feet. At a sign from the princess, her retinue of fairies and demons flew out of the building and up into the air with their royal mistress in their midst and vanished.

THE HIGGLEDY-PIGGLEDY PALACE

Sarah, the wife of the patriarch Abraham, and the great mother of the Jewish people, was the most beautiful woman who ever lived. Everybody who saw her marveled at the dazzling radiance of her countenance; they stood spellbound before the glorious light that shone in her eyes and the wondrous clearness of her complexion. This greatly troubled Abraham when he fled from Canaan to Egypt. It was disconcerting to have crowds of travelers gazing at his wife as if she were something more than human. Besides, he feared that the Egyptians would seize Sarah for the king's harem.

So, after much meditation, he concealed his wife in a big box. When he arrived at the Egyptian frontier, the customs officials asked him what it contained.

"Barley," he replied.

"You say that because the duty on barley is the lowest," they said. "The box must surely be packed with wheat."

"I will pay the duty on wheat," said Abraham, who was most anxious they should not open the box.

The officials were surprised, for, as a rule, people endeavored to avoid paying the duties.

"If you are so ready to pay the higher tax," they said, "the box must contain something of greater value. Perhaps it contains spices."

Abraham intimated his readiness to pay the duty on spices.

"Oh, Oh!" laughed the officers. "Here is a strange person ready to pay heavy dues. He must be anxious to conceal something--gold, perchance."

"I will pay the duty on gold," said Abraham, quietly.

The officers were now completely bewildered.

"Our highest duty," said their chief, "is on precious stones, and since you decline to open the box, we must demand the tax on the costliest gems."

"I will pay it," said Abraham, simply.

The officers could not understand this at all, and after consulting among themselves, they decided that the box must be opened.

"It may contain something highly dangerous," they argued.

Abraham protested, but he was arrested by the guards and the box forced open. When Sarah was revealed, the officials stepped back in amazement and admiration.

"Indeed, a rare jewel," said the chief.

It was immediately decided to send Sarah to the king. When Pharaoh beheld her, he was enraptured. She was simply dressed in the garments of a peasant woman, with no adornment and no jewels, and yet the king thought he had never seen a woman so entrancingly beautiful. When he saw Abraham, however, his brow clouded.

"Who is this man?" he demanded of Sarah.

Fearing that he might be imprisoned, or even put to death if she acknowledged him as her husband, Sarah replied that he was her brother.

Pharaoh felt relieved. He smiled on Abraham and greeted him pleasantly.

"Thy sister is exceeding fair to gaze upon," he said, "and comely of form. She hath bewitched me by her matchless charm. She shall become the favorite of my harem. I will recompense thee well for thy loss of her. Thou shalt be loaded with gifts."

Abraham was too wise to betray the anger that surged in his heart.

"Courage, my beloved," he whispered to Sarah. "The good God will not forsake us."

He made pretense of agreeing to Pharaoh's suggestion, and the chief steward of the king gave him an abundant store of gold and silver and jewels, also sheep and oxen and camels. Abraham was conducted to a beautiful palace, where many slaves attended him and bowed before him, for one on whom the monarch had showered favors was a great man in the land of Pharaoh. Left alone, Abraham began to pray most devoutly.

Meanwhile, Sarah was led into a gorgeous apartment where the queen's own attendants were ordered to array her in the richest of the royal garments. Then she was brought before Pharaoh who dismissed all the attendants.

"I desire to be alone with thee," said the king to Sarah. "I have much to say to thee, and I long to feast my eyes on those features of beauty rare."

But Sarah shrank from him. To her, he appeared ugly and loathsome. His smile was a vicious leer, and his voice sounded like a harsh croak.

"Fear not," he said, trying to speak tenderly and kindly. "I will do thee no harm. Nay, I will load thee with honors. I will grant any request that thou makest."

"Then let me go hence," said Sarah, quickly. "I desire naught but that thou shouldst permit me to depart with my brother."

"Thou jestest," said Pharaoh. "That cannot be. I will make thee queen," he cried, passionately and he made a move toward her.

"Stop!" cried Sarah. "If thou approachest one step nearer. . ."

Pharaoh interrupted with a laugh. To threaten a king was so funny that he could not refrain from a hoarse cackle. But Sarah had become suddenly silent. She was looking not at him, but behind him. Pharaoh turned, but observed nothing. He could not see what Sarah saw--a figure, a spirit, clutching a big stick.

"Come," said the king, "be not foolish. I cannot be angry with a creature so fair as thou art. But it is not meet--nay, it is not wise--to utter threats to one who wears a crown."

Sarah made no reply. She was no longer afraid. She knew that her prayers, and those of Abraham, had been answered, and that no harm would befall her. Pharaoh mistook her silence and advanced toward her. As he did so, however, he felt a tremendous blow on the head. He was stunned for a moment. On recovering himself he looked all round the room, but could see nothing. Sarah continued to stand motionless.

"Strange," muttered Pharaoh. "I--I thought some one had entered the room."

Again he moved toward Sarah, and once more he received a staggering blow--this time on the shoulder. It was only by a great effort of will that he did not cry out in pain. He concluded he must have been seized by some sudden illness, but after a moment he felt better and bravely tried to smile at Sarah.

"I--I just thought of something most important," said he, attempting to offer some explanation for nearly toppling over in an undignified manner. He stood nearer to Sarah and began to raise his hand to touch her.

"If thou layest but a finger on me, it will be at thy peril," exclaimed Sarah, her eyes flashing angrily.

"Pshaw!" he cried, losing patience, and he raised his hand.

This time the cudgel of the spirit invisible to Pharaoh did not strike him: it came down gently and rested lightly on the king's outstretched arm. And Pharaoh could not move it. He grew pale and trembled.

"Art thou a witch?" he gasped, at last.

Sarah was so angry when she heard this insult that she flashed a signal with her eyes to the spirit, and the latter plied his cudgel lustily about the king's head and shoulders, making the monarch break out in most unkingly howls of pain.

"Thy pardon, thy pardon, I crave," he managed to scream. "I mean not what I said. I am ill--very ill. My body aches. My arm is paralyzed."

The cudgeling ceased and Pharaoh was able to move his arm. He writhed in agony, for he was bruised all over. He rushed hastily away, saying he would return on the morrow. Sarah found herself locked in, but she was not again disturbed.

Pharaoh, however, had further adventures. The spirit was in merry mood and had a night's entertainment at the king's expense. No sooner did the king lie down upon his bed than the spirit tilted it and sent him sprawling on the floor. Whenever Pharaoh tried to lie down the same thing happened. He went from one room to another, but all efforts at rest were unavailing. Every bed rejected him and every chair and couch did the same, although when he commanded others to lie down they did so quite comfortably. He tried lying down with one of his attendants, but while the latter was able to remain undisturbed, Pharaoh found himself bodily lifted, stood upon his head, spun around and then rolled over on the ground.

His physicians could provide no remedy, his magicians--hastily summoned from their own slumbers--could afford no explanation, and Pharaoh spent a terrible night wandering from room to room and up and down the corridors, where the corners seemed to go out of their way to bump against him and the stairs seemed to go down when he wanted to walk up, and vice-versa. Such a higgledy-piggeldy palace was never seen. Worse still, with the first streak of dawn he noticed that he was smitten with leprosy.

Hastily he sent for Abraham and said: "Who and what thou art I know not. Thou and thy sister have brought a plague upon me. I desired to make her my queen, but now I say to you: Rid me of this leprosy and get thee hence with thy sister. I will bestow riches on ye, but get ye gone, and speedily."

With a magic jewel which he wore on his breast, Abraham restored Pharaoh to health, and then departed with Sarah. These final words he said to Pharaoh:

"Sarah is not my sister, but my wife. I give thee this warning. Should thy descendants at any time seek to persecute our descendants, then will our God, He, the One God of the universe, surely punish the king with plague again."

And, many years afterward, as you read in the Bible, the prediction came true.

THE RED SLIPPER

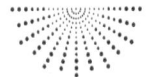

*R*osy-red was a sweet little girl, with beautiful blue eyes, soft pink cheeks and glorious ruddy-gold hair of the tinge that artists love to paint. Her mother died the day she was born, but her grandmother looked after her with such tender care that Rosy-red regarded her as her mother. She was very happy, was Rosy-red. All day long she sang, as she tripped gaily about the house or the woods that surrounded it, and so melodious was her voice that the birds gathered on the trees to listen to her and to encourage her to continue, by daintily chirruping whenever she ceased.

Merrily Rosy-red performed all the little duties her grandmother called upon her to do, and on festivals she was allowed to wear a delightful pair of red leather slippers, her father's gift to her on her first birthday. Now, although neither she nor her father knew it, they were magic slippers which grew larger as her feet grew.

Rosy-red was only a child and so did not know that slippers don't usually grow. Her grandmother knew the secret of the slippers, but she did not tell, and her father had become too moody and too deeply absorbed in his own thoughts and affairs to notice anything.

One day--Rosy-red remembered it only too sadly--she returned from the woods to find her grandmother gone and three strange women in the house. She stopped suddenly in the midst of her singing and her cheeks turned pale, for she did not like the appearance of the strangers.

"Who are you?" she asked.

"I am your new mother," answered the eldest of the three, "and these are my daughters, your two new sisters."

Rosy-red trembled with fear. They were all three so ugly, and she began to cry.

Her new sisters scolded her for that and would have beaten her had not her father appeared. He spoke kindly, telling her he had married again, because he was lonely and that her step-mother and step-sisters would be good to her. But Rosy-red knew different. She hastened away to her own little room and hid her slippers of which she was very proud.

"They have turned my dear granny out of doors; they will take from me my beautiful slippers," she sobbed.

After that, Rosy-red sang no more. She became a somber girl and a drudge. The birds could not understand. They followed her through the woods, but she was silent, as if she had been stricken dumb, and her eyes always seemed eager to be shedding tears. Also, she was too busy to notice her feathered friends.

She had to collect firewood for the home, to draw water from the well and struggle along with the heavy bucket whose weight made her arms and her back ache with pain. Sometimes, too, her white arms were scarred with bruises, for her cruel and selfish step-sisters did not hesitate to beat her. Often they went out to parties, or to dances, and on these occasions she had to act as their maid and help them to dress. Rosy-red did not mind; she was only happy when they were out of the house. Then only did she sing softly to herself, and the birds came to listen.

And thus many unhappy years passed away.

Once, when her father was away from home, her step-sisters went off to a wedding dance. They told her not to forget to draw water from the well, and warned her that if she forgot, as she did the last time, they would beat her without mercy when they returned.

So Rosy-red, tired though she was, went out in the darkness to draw water. She lowered the bucket, but the cord broke and the pail fell to the bottom of the well. She ran back home for a long stick with a hook at the end of it to recover the bucket, and as she put it into the water she sang:

> *Swing and sweep till all does cling*
> *And to the surface safely bring.*

Now it so happened that a sleeping jinn dwelt at the bottom of the well. He could only be awakened by a spell, and although Rosy-red did not know it, the words she uttered, which she had once heard her granny use, were the spell.

The jinn awoke, and he was so delighted with the sweet voice that he promptly decided to help the girl whom he saw peering down into the water. He fastened the bucket to the stick and, taking some jewels from a treasure of which he was the guardian, he put them inside.

"Oh, how beautiful," cried Rosy-red when she saw the glittering gems. "They are ever so much nicer than those my sisters put on to go to the ball."

Then she sat thinking for a while and a bright idea came into her head.

"I will give these jewels to my sisters," she said. "Perhaps they will be kinder to me."

She waited impatiently until the sisters re-turned from the dance and immediately told them. For a moment they were too dazed to speak when they saw the sparkling precious stones. Then they looked meaningly at one another and asked how she came by them. Rosy told them of the words she had sung.

"Ah, we thought so," said the sisters, to her horror. "The jewels are ours. We hid them in the well for safety. You have stolen them."

In vain Rosy-red protested. Her sisters would not listen. They beat her severely, told her to hurry off to bed, and then, snatching the bucket, they hurried off to the well. They lowered the bucket and sang the words that Rosy-red had sung. At least they thought they sang; but their voices were harsh. The sleeping jinn awoke again, but he did not like the croaking sound the sisters made.

"Ha, ha!" he laughed. "I will teach you to disturb my sleep with hideous noises and shall punish such pranks played on me. Here are some more croakers," and he filled the bucket with slimy toads and frogs.

The sisters were so enraged that they ran back home and dragged poor Rosy-red from her bed.

"You cat, you thief," screamed one.

"You cheat," exclaimed the other. "Off you go. Not another day can you remain in this house."

Rosy-red was too much taken by surprise to say anything. It was an outrage to turn her out of her father's house while he was away on a journey, but the thought came to her that she could hardly be less happy living alone in the woods.

She had only time to snatch her pretty red slippers, and as soon as she was out of sight of the house she put them on. It made her feel less miserable. The sun was now rising and when its rays shone on her she began to sing. With her old friends, the birds, twittering all about her, she felt quite happy.

On and on she walked, much farther into the woods than ever before. When she grew tired there was always a pleasant shady nook where she could rest; when she became hungry, there were fruit trees in abundance; and when she was thirsty she always came to a spring of clear, fresh water. The magic slippers guided her. All day long she wandered, and when toward evening she noticed her slippers were muddy she took them off to clean. And then darkness fell. It began to rain and she grew frightened. She crouched under a tree until she noticed a light some short distance away. She got up and walked toward it.

When quite close, she saw that the light came from a cave dwelling. An old woman came out to meet her. It was her grandmother, but so many years had passed that Rosy-red did not recognize her. Granny, however, at once knew her. "Come in, my child, and take shelter from the rain," she said kindly, and Rosy-red was only too glad to accept the invitation.

The inside of the cave was quite cosy, and Rosy-red, who was almost completely exhausted, quickly fell fast asleep. She awoke with a start.

"My pretty red slippers," she cried. "Where are they?"

She put her hand in the pocket of her tattered dress, but could only find one.

"I must have lost the other," she sobbed. "I must go out and look for it."

"No, no," said granny. "You cannot do that. A storm is raging."

Rosy-red peered out through the door of the cave and drew back in fear as she saw the lightning flash and heard the thunder rolling. She sobbed herself to sleep again, and this time was awakened by voices. She feared it might be her sisters who had discovered her hiding place and had come to drag her forcibly back home again. So she crept into a corner of the cave and listened intently.

A man was speaking.

"Know you to whom this red slipper belongs?" he was asking. "I found it in the woods."

Rosy-red was on the point of rushing out to regain her lost slipper when her granny's voice--very loud on purpose that she should hear--restrained her.

"No, no, I know not," she repeated again and again, and at length the man departed.

Granny came back into the cave and said, "I am sorry, Rosy-red, but for aught I knew, he might be a messenger from your cruel sisters; and, of course, I cannot let anyone take you back to them."

Next day, the man called again, this time with several attendants. Again, Rosy-red concealed herself.

"I am a chieftain's son, and wealthy," said the man. "I must find the wearer of this shoe. Only a graceful and beautiful girl can wear such a dainty slipper."

Rosy-red did not know whether to be more frightened or pleased, when her granny told her the man was very handsome and of noble bearing.

Day after day he came, each time with more retainers, and, finally, he arrived mounted on a richly caparisoned camel with a hundred and one followers, all mounted as he was.

"The girl I seek is here," he said. "Deny it no longer. My servants have scoured the woods and the whole neighborhood. One is prepared to swear he heard a young girl singing yesterday."

Rosy-red saw that concealment was no longer possible. She liked the man's voice, and she stepped out bravely, wearing her one slipper.

The stranger, bowing low before her, held out the other, and Rosy-red took it and put it on. It fitted perfectly.

"Many girls have tried to put on that shoe," said the young man. "but all have failed. And I have sworn to make the wearer my bride. I am a chieftain's son, and thou shalt be a princess."

So Rosy-red left the cave with her granny, and mounting a camel was led through the woods to her new home where she knew naught but happiness and the days of her sufferings were quite forgotten. And always she wore her magic red slippers.

THE STAR-CHILD

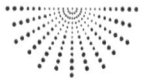

When Abraham was born, his father, Terah, who was one of the chief officers of King Nimrod, gave a banquet to a large number of his friends. He entertained them most sumptuously, and the merriest of the guests was the chief of the king's magicians. He was an old man, exceedingly fond of wine, and he drank deeply. The feast lasted throughout the night, and the gray dawn of early morning appeared in the sky before Terah's friends thought of rising from the table.

Suddenly the old magician jumped to his feet.

"See," he cried, excitedly, pointing through the open door to the sky. "See yon bright star in the east. It flashes across the heavens."

The others looked, but said they could see nothing.

"Fools," shouted the old man, "ye may not see, but I do. I, the wisest of the king's magicians and astrologers, tell you it is an omen. See how the brilliant star darts across the sky! It has swallowed a smaller star, and another, even a third, yet a fourth. It is an omen, I say, a portent that bodes ill. And, moreover," he added, growing still more excited, "it is an omen connected with the birth of the little son of Terah."

"Nonsense," cried Terah.

"Talk not to me of nonsense," said the magician, sternly. "I must hasten to inform the king."

Hurriedly he left the house of Terah, followed by the other magicians, some of whom now said they also had seen a star swallow four others.

They did not think it wise to contradict their chief, although he had drunk a great deal of wine and could not walk steadily.

King Nimrod was awakened from his sleep, and his magicians appeared before him.

"O King, live for ever," said the chief, by way of salute. "Grave indeed is the news that has led us to disturb thee in thy slumbers. This night a son has been born unto thy officer, Terah, and with the coming of the dawn a warning has appeared to us in the skies. I, the chief of thy magicians, did observe a brilliant star rise in the east and dart across the heavens and swallow four smaller stars."

"We observed it, too," said the other magicians.

"And what means this?" inquired the king.

"It means," said the chief magician, mysteriously, "that this star-child will destroy other children, that his descendants will conquer thine. Take warning. Purchase this child from thy officer, Terah, and slay it so that it may not grow up a danger to thee."

"Thy advice pleases me," said the cruel king.

In vain Terah protested. King Nimrod would not disregard the warning of his magicians, but he consented to give Terah three days in which to deliver up the child. Sad at heart Terah returned home, and on the second day told his wife the terrible news.

"We must not allow our little son, Abraham, to be slain," she said. "If he is to become great he must live. I have a plan. King Nimrod will not be satisfied unless a child is slain. Therefore, take thou the child of a slave to him and tell him it is Abraham. He will not know the difference. And so that the trick shall not be discovered, take our child away and hide it for a time."

Terah thought this an excellent idea, and he carried it out. The sick child of a slave, which was born only a few hours before Abraham, was taken to King Nimrod who killed it with his own hands, and Terah's little boy was secretly carried by his nurse to a cave in a forest. There Abraham was carefully nurtured and brought up.

From time to time Abraham was visited by his father and mother, and not until he was ten years old did they think it safe to bring him from the cave in the forest to their home. Even then they deemed it best to be careful. Their elder son, Haran, was a maker of idols and Abraham became his helper without Haran being told it was his brother.

Abraham, the star-child, was a strange little boy. He did not believe in the idols.

"I worship the sun by day and the moon and the stars by night," he said to Haran.

"There are times when you cannot see the sun by day, nor the moon and stars by night," said Haran, "but you can always have your idol with you."

This troubled little Abraham for a while, but one day he came running to his brother and said, "I have made a discovery. I shall no longer worship the sun, nor the moon, nor the stars. There must be some mighty power behind them that orders them to shine, the sun by day and the moon and stars by night. That great power shall be my God."

Abraham asked all sorts of queer questions of his father. "Who made the sun and the moon and the stars?" he asked.

"I know not," replied Terah.

"I have asked all your idols, your gods. and they answer not," said Abraham.

"They cannot speak," said Terah.

"Then why do you pray to them and worship them?" persisted the boy.

Terah did not answer. Abraham asked his mother, but she could only tell him that the gods who created everything were with them in the house.

"But Haran made those silly things of wood and clay," said Abraham, and at last they refused to answer his awkward questions.

Mostly he stood at the door of the house, gazing at the sky as if trying to read the secrets behind the sun and stars.

"Thou shouldst have been placed with an astrologer," said Haran to him one day. "Thou art a child of the stars." Terah heard this and was angry with Haran, for he feared that the secret of the child's birth might be betrayed.

"I know not why my father keeps thee here," said Haran afterward to Abraham. "Thou art becoming lazy. I have worked enough this day and will go out to the woods to watch the hunting. Stay thou here. Perchance a purchaser may come. Be heedful and obtain good payment for the idols."

Not long after Haran left, an old man entered the shop and said he wished to buy an idol.

"I dropped my idol on the ground yesterday and it broke," he said. "I must have a stronger one."

"Certainly thou must have a god so strong that naught can break it," answered Abraham. "Tell me, how old art thou?"

"Full sixty years, boy," replied the man.

"And yet thou hast not reached years of wisdom," said Abraham. "See how easy it is to break thy gods," and he took a stick and smashed one of the idols with a single blow.

The old man fled from the shop horrified.

Next, a woman entered.

"I am too poor to have an idol of my own," she said. "Therefore, I have brought a little food as an offering to one of the many gods here."

"Offer it to any idol that pleases thee," said Abraham, with a laugh.

The woman placed it before the smallest idol.

"This idol is small and surly," said the boy. "It does not accept thy offering," and he raised his stick and smashed it.

"Try a bigger idol with thy offering," he said, and the woman did so.

"Thou also hast no manners," said Abraham, addressing the god; "eat, or I shall smash thee to pieces."

The idol, of course, did not eat, and so Abraham broke it, and the woman rushed out into the street in great alarm.

Abraham tried all the idols in turn with the food, and as each was unable to eat, he broke them all except the largest. Before this idol, which was as tall as a man, he paused. Then, laughing loudly, he placed the stick which he had used in the idol's hand.

By this time, a crowd, attracted by the cries of the old man and the woman, had gathered at the door.

"What hast thou done?" they demanded, angrily.

"I? Nothing," answered Abraham. "See, the largest idol holds in its hand a big stick. It seems to me that he has been angry and has killed all the others. Ask him why he did this."

The people stood bewildered until Terah and Haran returned.

"What is the meaning of this?" they asked, pointing to the broken idols.

"Oh! Such fun," replied Abraham. "There has been a fight here. A woman brought a food offering to the gods, and they quarrelled because they all wanted it. So the big fellow here got angry, and, taking up the stick which you see he still holds, he beat the others and smashed them to bits."

"Absurd!" cried Haran. "The idols cannot do these things."

"Ask the big fellow to strike me if I have told lies," returned Abraham.

"Cease your nonsense," commanded his father.

"What funny gods yours are," said Abraham, musingly, standing before the big idol. "Do you think he will hit me if I smack his face?"

Before anybody could stop him, he smacked the idol's face and then knocked off its head with the stick.

Some of the people ran off to the palace, and soon came an order from King Nimrod that the idol-breaker should be brought before him. Abraham, Haran and Terah were seized by the guards and marched off to the palace.

"Which of you broke the idols?" asked the king, angrily.

"I did, because they were rude and would not accept the offering," said Abraham. "How can they be gods if they have no sense?"

"Not altogether a foolish remark," said Nimrod, smiling. "If idols please thee not, then worship fire which has the power to consume."

"Fire itself can be quenched by water," replied Abraham.

"Then worship water," returned Nimrod. "But water is absorbed by the clouds," said the boy.

"And clouds are blown by the wind," said Nimrod.

"Man can withstand the force of the wind." said Abraham.

"So he will talk all day long, this child of the stars," exclaimed Haran.

"Child of the stars!" said the chief magician. "Now I understand. O king, this must be no other than the child of Terah against whom, at his birth, we warned your majesty. The message of the stars has come true. He has dared to destroy our gods. Soon he will destroy us."

"Is this, in truth, the child of the stars?" asked Nimrod, of Terah, but the latter did not answer.

"It is in truth, your majesty," said Haran. "I have long suspected it."

"Then why didst thou not inform me?" exclaimed the king in a rage. "I will test this star-child with the power of my god, fire. And thou, Haran, for thy neglect, must also suffer. Guards, let them be bound and cast into the furnace to which I pray daily. Terah, thou art their father. I can forgive thee; thou wilt suffer sufficiently in losing both thy sons to my god."

The fire was made so hot that the men who endeavored to cast Abraham and Haran into the flames were caught and burned to death. Twelve men in all perished before Terah's sons were thrown into the furnace. Haran was burned to ashes at once, but to the surprise of the vast crowd that stood at a safe distance, Abraham walked unharmed in the flames, the fetters which bound him having been consumed.

When King Nimrod saw this, he trembled.

"Come forth, boy," he cried to Abraham, "and I will pardon thee."

"Bid your men take me out," he answered.

All who approached the terrific fire, however, were burned to death, and at last when Nimrod said he would bow down before Abraham's God the boy came forth unharmed.

All the people bowed down before the boy who told them to rise, saying, "Worship not me, but the true God who dwells in Heaven beyond the sun and the stars and whose glory is everywhere."

King Nimrod loaded the boy with presents and bade him return home in peace.

ABI FRESSAH'S FEAST

There was not in the whole city of Bagdad a greedier man than Abi Fressah, and you may be sure he was not popular. It was not that he was rich and refused to give heed to the needs of the poor. He was, in truth, a merchant in moderately affluent circumstances, and he did not withhold charity from the deserving; but he was a man of enormous appetite and did not scruple to descend to trickery to secure an invitation to a meal.

So skilful, indeed, did he become in wheedling these favors from his friends and from those with whom he traded, that he devoted the major portion of each day to feeding and left himself little time to attend to his business affairs. Moreover, he grew unpleasantly fat. His face was red and bloated with much wine drinking. He was not a nice person to look upon at all, and those who had aforetime been his friends came to the conclusion that the day had arrived when he should be taught a severe lesson.

And so it came to pass that when Abi Fressah was standing in the bazaar at the hour of the mid-day meal and eagerly scanning the crowd to discover some acquaintance whom he could induce to ask him to dinner, he saw Ben Maslia, one of the wealthiest and most generous of men in Bagdad.

"Ah, my excellent friend," Abi cried, warmly greeting Ben Maslia, "'tis almost an eternity since nay unworthy eyes were cast upon thy pleasant countenance. Peace be on thee and thine unto the end of days."

"Also to thee," returned Ben Maslia.

"And whence comest thou? And whither goest thou, oh most hospitable friend?" Abi Fressah asked these questions hastily, his beady eyes searching the other's face hungrily for a sign upon which he could seize to invite himself to a meal. "It is the hour of the mid-day meal. Goest thou, perchance, to thy pious home?"

"Thither go I," said Ben Maslia.

"My path lies in the same direction," said Abi Fressah. "It will be pleasant to walk together. Come," and he grasped Ben Maslia by the arm.

"It is kind of thee, friend Abi Fressah," rejoined the other, "but I have built me a new abode on the other side of the city."

Abi Fressah's face fell for a moment, but he was clever enough to take advantage of the news.

"A new dwelling erected by the wealthy Ben Maslia," he said, winningly, "must be a building of magnificence, worth seeing."

"Indeed it is as thou sayest," cried the other enthusiastically, and forthwith he launched into a lavish description of his residence.

Abi Fressah grew impatient when Ben Maslia began to describe each room in detail, his hunger increased when, in glowing words, his friend painted the gorgeous dining-room, and his mouth watered at the information that the cellars were stocked with a thousand bottles of wine.

"Blessings on thee and thy wine-cellar and thy house," murmured Abi Fressah, when he could get in a word. "I have no business of consequence to transact this afternoon. I could not pay thee a better compliment than to spend it examining thy treasures."

"Of a certainty thou couldst not," assented the other, to his great glee.

"Then let us proceed," said Abi Fressah.

So they set out, Ben Maslia still continuing his glowing account of his wonderful house.

"It must be as spacious as a palace," put in Abi Fressah.

"Thou speakest truth," agreed Ben Maslia. "I will illustrate to thee the vast expanse of my new
residence."

He stopped in his walk, measured one hundred paces in the street, and intimated that this represented the width of the central courtyard.

Abi Fressah was overwhelmed with surprise, but he was growing momentarily hungrier, and it was with difficulty he could restrain his impatience.

"Yes, yes," he said, "I would fain gaze upon the outer door of thy dwelling."

"Such an outer door," said Ben Maslia, "hast thou never seen. Its width. . ." and again he began to measure the street to indicate its dimensions.

"And further," he added, calmly, either failing to notice, or deliberately overlooking Abi Fressah's growing distress, "its shape and design are . . .!" and he dragged the other through several streets until he found a door to which he could point as being not altogether unlike his own.

"But I weary thee," he said, suddenly, as if regretful of the time he had wasted.

"Nay, nay, not at all," Abi Fressah assured him, although he was inwardly fuming at the delay.

"Thy descriptions delight me immeasurably. Thou hast not yet unfolded to me the wonders of thy dining-room."

Thereupon Ben Maslia took up the tale of the dining-room and its furniture, and he dragged his companion half a mile out of their path to show him the furniture emporium where he had purchased the tables and the couches. Then he retraced his steps to point out a building from which he had borrowed certain ideas of decoration.

Abi Fressah's fat body was unused to such exertion. He perspired freely, his legs tottered beneath him, and his tongue was parched. He was really very uncomfortable, and the pangs of hunger from which he suffered were not lessened when Ben Maslia stopped outside a restaurant to speak to a friend who was just going in.

The conversation was prolonged, and all the time Abi Fressah's nose was tickled by the smell of the cooking. He endured agonies, especially when the friend invited Ben Maslia to dine with him, and Ben Maslia, after a few moment's hesitation, firmly declined.

"I must apologize to thee for this delay," said Ben Maslia, when at length he left his friend, "but the matter was urgent. I will make up to thee by the magnificence of the feast."

Abi Fressah thanked him cordially for his consideration, but his pain was intense when Ben Maslia insisted on giving him fullest particulars of all the dishes he would enjoy.

"Yes, yes," Abi kept saying, but Ben Maslia stayed his interruptions.

"Thy dwelling is far from the center of the city," Abi Fressah managed to say at last.

"That is a virtue," commented Ben Maslia, and he followed it up with the advice given to him by a renowned physician that a house was healthiest when it stood alone, away from the busy haunts of men. To all this and more, Abi Fressah was compelled to listen. His whole fat body ached with weariness, he was tortured by a raging thirst, and he fancied he felt himself growing thinner--so fearfully hungry was he.

The sun was sinking when at last they reached the house, and Abi Fressah was afraid for a moment that his host would enlarge upon its architecture. To his relief, however, they entered straightway, and Ben Maslia said to him, "Thou must be fatigued after thy walk. Rest awhile."

Abi Fressah was truly grateful, and taking off his shoes he stretched himself on a comfortable couch. He dozed for a while, but was awakened by the noise of clattering dishes and the smell of savory cooking. He almost forgot his unpleasant afternoon in the prospect of the coming feast, but Ben Maslia came not. Abi Fressah soon felt angry. He could not restrain himself from banging a big brass gong to summon a servant. But although he banged several times, no servant answered the call. Abi Fressah nearly shed tears in his despair.

Suddenly Ben Maslia appeared before him.

"I thought I would give thee ample rest," he said suavely. "Come, we must perform our ablutions."

Abi Fressah would have preferred to have dispensed with this ceremony, but he could not offend his host by declining to conform to the custom of the period. Ben Maslia led the way to the bath-chamber, and there they spent quite an hour. Then, thoroughly refreshed, the host said, "Now I will show thee the wonders and beauties of my domain."

Abi Fressah was almost stupefied with hunger, but he had to permit himself to be led through each room and to hear again the praises that had already been poured into his ears all the afternoon. Only the smell of the cooking fortified his spirit and enabled him to undergo the ordeal. He seemed to wake up from a stupor when his host opened a door and exclaimed, "This is the feasting-chamber."

A scene of splendor burst upon the eyes of Abi Fressah. He rubbed his hands in glee and was ready to forget and forgive the discomforts of the past few hours. The dining-room presented a magnificent appearance, with its gorgeous hangings, its many lamps, and its marble floor. But these things Abi Fressah scarcely noted. His gaze was promptly directed on the table.

It was spread with the most sumptuous repast that ever he had seen. There were dishes upon dishes of tasty sweetmeats, huge platters of luscious fruits, many bottles of wine, and covered bowls from which arose the most appetizing aroma. Abi Fressah's mouth began to twitch and his eyes glowed. He moved forward to a seat.

"Good friend," said his host, "let me first introduce to your notice my staff of servants."

He clapped his hands, and immediately, in quite startling fashion, a dozen servants stepped from behind the hangings which had hidden them and bowed before their master. With a dozen attendants to wait upon him, Abi Fressah saw that he was going to enjoy a meal worthy of the occasion. He looked upon the slaves with satisfaction.

"Note, my worthy Abi Fressah," said Ben Maslia, "that this is no ordinary retinue of servants. Each one comes from a different part of the known world. Rosh, the big man there, head of them all, is the only native of Bagdad. He has an interesting history. He has been in my service since his birth. His father was likewise in the service of my sainted father, and his grandfather . . . But let that suffice. I would not imprison thy appetite longer. Sheni--that is the second servant, the big black Nubian there--bring hither the first dish."

Sheni took up one of the dishes from the table and placed himself by the side of his master.

"Stands he not well?" asked Ben Maslia, in admiring tones. "He is a descendant of kings. In ancient days his ancestors sat on a throne and ruled over a huge territory beyond the deserts of Africa. I obtained him during my journey in that country. And on that occasion I discovered this beautiful rug in a shop in Cairo."

Saying which, Ben Maslia rose from his seat and fingered lovingly one of the hangings of the room. Abi Fressah did not rise. He was trying to keep his temper. The dish which Sheni held so tantalizingly under his very nose made him mad with hunger and desire.

But Ben Maslia took no heed. He began to dilate upon the virtues of another piece of tapestry.

"This," he said, "I bought in the famous bazaar of Damascus. It is hundreds of years old. And in that city, too, I became possessed of my third servant, Shelishi there, a true-born son of the Holy Land and the keeper of my camels. Our meeting was an adventure . . ."

Abi Fressah was not listening. This was beyond endurance. He felt that soon he would collapse in a faint on the floor. And still Ben Maslia droned on. There was a servant from China and also a cunningly wrought vase from that land; a brown page boy in a red turban from India from which land his host had also brought the lamp standing in the center of the table and some of the flowers which adorned the room.

"You would not guess," he was saying, "that many of these blooms are

ABI FRESSAH'S FEAST | 49

not natural. They are artificial but mixed so skillfully with the real that even experts would be deluded."

By this time Abi Fressah was beyond the power of speech. Two or three times, he tried to speak but could not. He was really too weak. Never in his life before had he been so hungry, so tortured. It was some time, however, before Ben Maslia noticed his plight.

"Art thou ill?" he exclaimed. "That grieves me. But, fortunately, I have in the house an experienced apothecary who can apply leeches and relieve thee of foul blood."

"No, no," pleaded the unhappy Abi Fressah, finding his tongue at this dismal prospect.

"Perchance a glass of rare cordial will revive thee," said Ben Maslia, taking one of the bottles from the table.

Abi Fressah managed to gasp the word "Yes," and Rosh held a goblet into which Ben Maslia poured a rich, red fluid.

"Drink this," he said kindly, holding the cup to his guest's lip.

"At last," thought Abi Fressah, as he opened his mouth.

The next moment he sprang from his stool with astonishing agility, spluttering and cursing. The liquid was bitter in the extreme, the taste it left in his mouth most horrid.

"Now I know I have been hoodwinked," he screamed in rage, and he dashed toward the outer door.

"Stay, stay--what ails thee?" cried Ben Maslia.

"Stop, stop," echoed the servants, as Abi Fressah commenced to run.

The cry was taken up in the street by those who saw a fat man panting along in the darkness, pursued by a number of servants.

"Stop thief!" was the cry of one man in his excitement. The town guards heard, and without any ado they seized Abi Fressah and hauled him off to the jail. In vain he begged for mercy and struggled for freedom.

"If thou wilt not behave, we shall use force," the guards said, and they beat him with staves.

At the jail, Abi Fressah was flung into a cell, and there, on a bed of straw on the ground, he spent a horrible, sleepless night. He ached in every bone in his body, he was bruised all over, and his hunger was such that he felt he had never eaten in his life. His reflections were sad, as you may well imagine, and they led him to a vow that never again would he seek the hospitality of his friends. He realized at last that he had made himself obnoxious and had been cleverly and deservedly well punished.

Even yet his sufferings were not at an end, for next morning, when he was released and sent for his physician, the latter prescribed a diet of gruel and barley water for a whole week!

THE BEGGAR KING

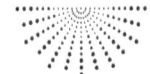

  Proud King Hagag sat on his throne in state, and the high priest, standing by his side, read from the Holy Book, as was his daily custom. He read these words: "For riches are not for ever: and doth the crown endure to every generation?"
  "Cease!" cried the king. "Who wrote those words?"
  "They are the words of the Holy Book," answered the high priest.
  "Give me the book," commanded the king.
  With trembling hands the high priest placed it before his majesty. King Hagag gazed earnestly at the words that had been read, and he frowned. Raising his hand, he tore the page from the book and threw it to the ground.
  "I, Hagag, am king," he said, "and all such passages that offend me shall be torn out."
  He flung the volume angrily from him while the high priest and all his courtiers looked on in astonishment.
  "I have heard enough for today," he said. "Too long have I delayed my hunting expedition. Let the horses be got ready."
  He descended from the throne, stalked haughtily past the trembling figure of the high priest, and went forth to the hunt. Soon he was riding furiously across an open plain toward a forest where a wild stag had been seen. A trumpet sounded the signal that the deer had been driven from its hiding place, and the king urged his horse forward to be the first in the chase. His majesty's steed was the swiftest in the land. Quickly it carried

him out of sight of his nobles and attendants. But the deer was surprisingly fleet and the king could not catch up with it. Coming to a river, the animal plunged in and swam across. Scrambling up the opposite bank its antlers caught in the branch of a tree, and the king, arriving at the river, gave a cry of joy.

"Now I have thee," he said. Springing from his horse and divesting himself of his clothing he swam across with naught but a sword.

As he reached the opposite bank, however, the deer freed itself from the tree and plunged into a thicket. The king, with his sword in his hand, followed quickly, but no deer could he see. Instead, he found, lying on the ground beyond the thicket, a beautiful youth clad in a deer-skin. He was panting as if after a long run. The king stood still in surprise and the youth sprang to his feet.

"I am the deer," he said. "I am a genii and I have lured thee to this spot, proud king, to teach thee a lesson for thy words this morning."

Before King Hagag could recover from his surprise the youth ran back to the river and swam across. Quickly he dressed himself in the king's clothes and mounted the horse just as the other hunters came up. They thought the genii was King Hagag and they halted before him.

"Let us return," said the genii. "The deer has crossed the river and has escaped."

King Hagag from the thicket on the opposite side watched them ride away and then flung himself on the ground and wept bitterly. There he lay until a wood-cutter found him.

"What do you here?" asked the man.

"I am King Hagag," returned the monarch.

"Thou art a fool," said the wood-cutter. "Thou art a lazy good-for-naught to talk so. Come, carry my bundle of sticks and I will give thee food and an old garment."

In vain the king protested. The wood-cutter only laughed the more, and at last, losing patience, he beat him and drove him away. Tired and hungry, and clad only in the rags which the wood-cutter had given him, King Hagag reached the palace late at night.

"I am King Hagag," he said to the guards, but roughly they bade him begone, and after spending a wretched night in the streets of the city, his majesty, next morning, was glad to accept some bread and milk offered to him by a poor old woman who took pity on him. He stood at a street corner not knowing what to do. Little children teased him; others took him for a beggar and offered him money. Later in the day he saw the genii ride through the streets on his horse. All the people bowed down before him and cried, "Long live the king!"

"Woe is me," cried Hagag, in his wretchedness. "I am punished for my sin in scoffing at the words of the Holy Book."

He saw that it would be useless for him to go to the palace again, and he went into the fields and tried to earn his bread as a laborer. He was not used to work, however, and but for the kindness of the very poorest he would have died of starvation. He wandered miserably from place to place until he fell in with some blind beggars who had been deserted by their guide. Joyfully he accepted their offer to take the guide's place.

Months rolled by, and one morning the royal heralds went forth and announced that "Good King Hagag" would give a feast a week from that day to all the beggars in the land.

From far and near came beggars in hundreds, to partake of the king's bounty, and Hagag stood among them, with his blind companions, in the courtyard of the palace waiting for his majesty to appear. He knew the place well, and he hung his head and wept.

"His majesty will speak to each one of you who are his guests today," cried a herald, and one by one they passed into the palace and stood before the throne. When it came to Hagag's turn, he trembled so much that he had to be supported by the guards.

The genii on the throne and Hagag looked long at each other.

"Art thou, too, a beggar?" said the genii.

"Nay, gracious majesty," answered Hagag with bent head. "I have sinned grievously and have been punished. I am but the servant of a troop of blind beggars to whom I act as guide."

The genii king signed to his courtiers that he desired to be left alone with Hagag. Then he said:

"Hagag, I know thee. I see that thou hast repented. It is well. Now canst thou resume thy rightful place."

"Gracious majesty," said Hagag, "I have learned humility and wisdom. The throne is not for me. The blind beggars need me. Let me remain in their service."

"It cannot be," said the genii. "I see that thou art truly penitent. Thy lesson is learned and my task is done. I will see that the blind beggars lack not."

With his own hands he placed the royal robes on Hagag and himself donned those of the beggar. When the courtiers returned they saw no difference. King Hagag sat on the throne again, and nowhere in the whole world was there a monarch who ruled more wisely or showed more kindness and sympathy to all his subjects.

THE QUARREL OF THE CAT AND DOG

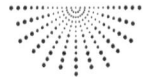

In the childhood of the world, when Adam named all the animals and ruled over them, the dog and the cat were the greatest good friends. They were inseparable chums in their recreations, faithful partners in their transactions, and devoted comrades in all their adventures, their pleasures and their sorrows. They lived together, shared each other's food and confided their secrets to none but themselves. It seemed that no possible difference would ever arise to cause trouble between them.

Then winter came. It was a new experience to them to feel the cold wind cutting through their skins and making them shiver. The dismal prospect of the leafless trees and the hard cold ground weighed heavily upon their hearts, and, worse still, there was less food. The scarcity grew serious, and hunger plunged them into unhappiness and despair. Doggie became melancholy, while Pussie grew peevish, then petulant, and finally developed a horrid temper.

"We can't go on like this," moaned the cat. "I think we had better dissolve partnership. We can't find enough to share when we are together, but separately we ought each to discover sufficient forage in our hunting."

"I think I can help you, because I am the stronger," said the dog.

Pussie did not contradict, but she thought the dog a bit of a fool and too good-natured. She knew herself to be sly and intended to rely on that quality for her future sustenance. Doggie was deeply hurt at Pussie's desire to end their happy compact, but he said quietly, "Of course, if you insist on parting, I will agree."

"It is agreed then," purred Pussie.

"Where will you go?" asked Doggie.

"To the house of Adam," promptly replied the cat, who had evidently made up her mind. "There are mice there. Adam will be grateful if I clear them away. I shall have food to eat."

"Very well," assented the dog. "I will wander further afield."

Then the cat said solemnly: "We must each take an oath never to cross the other's path. That is the proper way to terminate a business agreement. The serpent says so, and he is the wisest of all animals."

They put their right fore-paws together and gravely repeated an oath never to interfere with each other by going to the same place. Then they parted. Doggie trotted off sorrowfully with his head hanging down. Once he looked back, but Puss did not do so. She scampered off as fast as she could to the house of Adam.

"Father Adam," she cried, "I have come to be your slave. You are troubled with mice in the house. I can rid you of them, and I want nothing else for my services."

"Thou art welcome," said Father Adam, stroking Pussie's warm fur.

Puss rubbed her head against his feet, purred contentedly, and ran off to look for mice. She found plenty and soon grew fat and comfortable. Adam treated her kindly, and she soon forgot all about her former comrade.

Poor Doggie did not fare so well. Indeed, he had a rough time. He wandered aimlessly about over the frozen ground and could not find the slightest scrap of food. After three days, weary, paw-sore and dispirited, he came to a wolf's lair and begged for shelter. The wolf took pity on him, gave him some scraps of food, and permitted him to sleep in the lair. Doggie was most thankful, and sleeping with his ears on the alert, he heard stealthy footsteps in the night. He told the wolf.

"Drive the intruders away," said his host in a surly tone.

Doggie went out obediently to do so. But the marauders were wild animals and they nearly killed him. He was lucky to escape with his life. After bathing his wounds at a pool in the early morning he wandered all day long, but again could find nothing. Toward night, when he could scarcely drag his famished and wounded body along, he saw a monkey in a tree.

"Kind monkey," he pleaded, "give me shelter for the night. I am exhausted and starving."

"Go away, go away, go away," chattered the monkey, jumping and swinging swiftly from branch to branch, moving his lips quickly and opening and shutting his eyes comically. Doggie hesitated, and, to frighten him away, the monkey pulled cocoanuts from the tree and pelted him.

Poor Doggie crawled miserably away.

"What shall I do?" he moaned.

Hearing the bleating of some sheep, he made his way to them and asked them to take compassion on him.

"We will," they replied, "if you will keep watch over us and tell us when the wolf comes."

Doggie agreed willingly, and, after he had devoured some food, he stretched himself to sleep like a faithful watch-dog, with one eye open.

In the middle of the night he heard the wolves approaching, and, anxious to serve the sheep who had treated him kindly, he sprang to his feet and began to bark loudly. This aroused the sheep, who awoke and started to run in all directions. Some of them ran right into the pack of wolves and were killed and eaten. Poor Doggie was nearly heart-broken.

"It is my fault, my fault," he wailed. "I barked too soon. Oh, what an unhappy creature I am. I shall keep away from all animals now."

Once again he set off on his travels. Whenever he met an animal he ran off in the opposite direction. He had to make his journey by the loneliest paths and the most unfrequented routes, and the difficulty of finding food grew steadily greater. At last he grew so weak and thin that he hardly had strength to crawl and he had several narrow escapes from falling a prey to ferocious beasts.

One night he came to a house and begged a morsel of food. It was given, and during the night he woke the man and warned him that wild animals were making a raid. The man jumped up, seized his bow and arrow and drove the thieves away. Then he patted Doggie.

"Good dog," he said. "You are a wise animal. Stay with me always. You will find Father Adam kind."

"Father Adam!" cried Doggie, in alarm. "I must not stay here."

"Nonsense. I say you must," answered Adam, and Doggie was compelled to obey.

In the morning, Pussie learned that the dog had joined the household and she complained to Adam.

"The dog has violated the oath he swore not to come to the place where I am," she said.

"He did not know you were here," said Adam, desirous of maintaining peace. "He is very useful. I want him to remain. He won't hurt you. There is ample room for both."

"No, there isn't," said Puss spitefully, arching up her back and getting cross. "He broke his oath. He is a wicked creature. You dare not overlook his offense."

Poor Doggie stood dejectedly apart, with his tail between his legs.

"I didn't know it was Adam's house, and I was so hungry and miserable and tired," he said.

But Pussie would not be pacified. She thrust out her ugly claws and tried to scratch her former partner. The dog kept out of her way as much as possible, but she quarrelled with him at every opportunity, and at last he determined to tolerate her conduct no longer.

"I must leave you, Father Adam," he said. "Pussie is making my life unbearable."

"But I want you," said Adam.

"I'm sorry," said Doggie, firmly, "but it is really impossible for me to continue in your service. I've got another situation at the house of Seth. He wants me, too."

"Won't you make friends with Pussie?" asked Adam.

"With pleasure, if she will let me, but she won't."

"You blame each other," said Adam, losing patience. "I can't make you out. You look like quarrelling for ever."

Adam's words have proved true. Ever since that time the cat and dog have failed to agree, and Pussie will never consent to be friendly again with Doggie.

THE WATER-BABE

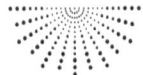

Floating in a basket on the River Nile, Princess Bathia, the daughter of Pharaoh, King of Egypt, found a tiny little water-babe. Princess Bathia was a widow and had no children, and she was so delighted that she took the child home to the palace and brought it up as her own. She called the babe Moses.

He was a pretty little boy, full of fun and frolic as he grew up, and he became a favorite with everybody in the palace. Even the cruel King Pharaoh, who had ordered that all the Hebrew boy babes should be drowned, loved to play with him. His ministers of state and magicians, however, frowned when they saw Moses, as soon as he could toddle and talk, making a play-mate of the king. They warned Pharaoh that it was dangerous to give a strange child such privileges, but Princess Bathia only laughed at them. So did her mother, the queen, and King Pharaoh took no notice.

When Moses was three years old, Princess Bathia gave a birthday party in his honor. It was really a big banquet and was attended by the king and queen and all the courtiers. Moses was seated at the head of the table and his eyes opened very wide with wonderment at everything he saw. It seemed such a ridiculous lot of solemn fuss to him. He would rather have played on the floor, or climbed on to the table, but of course they would not allow him.

"What does all this mean?" he asked of the king who was seated next to him. "Tell me," and he playfully pulled King Pharaoh's beard.

The courtiers looked on horrified, and Bilam, the chief magician, cried out, "Beware, O king, this is not play."

"Heed not these words, my father," said the princess. "Bilam is ever warning thee. If thou wert to take notice of all that he says, thou wouldst not have a moment's peace. Take our little babe on thy knee and play with him."

To please the princess, King Pharaoh did so, and Moses amused himself by playing with the glittering jewels on his majesty's robes. Then he looked up and stared hard at the king's head.

"What is that?" he asked, pointing.

"That is the royal crown," answered Pharaoh.

"No it is not; it is only a funny hat," replied Moses.

"Beware," chimed in Bilam, solemnly.

"Let me put the hat on," said Moses, reaching up his little hands, and before they could stop him, he had taken the crown from the king's head and had put it on his own.

Princess Bathia and the queen laughed merrily, but Bilam looked very grave.

"Your majesty," he said, in a voice trembling with passion, "this is not the foolish play of a babe. This child, remember, is not as other children. Came he not from the river? There is meaning in his action. Already does he seek to rob thee of thy royal crown. 'Tis a portent of evil."

Pharaoh thoughtfully stroked his beard. "What sayeth Reuel?" he asked, turning to his second chief magician.

"I say the child is but a babe and that this action means nothing," answered Reuel.

The queen and the princess agreed with Reuel, who was their favorite, but Bilam would not allow the matter to pass lightly.

"I, Bilam, am chief of thy counselors," he said, "and deeply learned in the mysteries of signs and portents. There is a meaning in all things. Remember, O King, this child is of the Hebrews, and escaped thy decree. This play of his hath a meaning. Should he be permitted to grow up, he will rebel against thee and seek to destroy thy rule. Let him be judged, O king."

"Thy words are wise," said Pharaoh, who was himself annoyed with Moses, and he ordered three judges to try the child for his offence.

Moses thought it was a new game and he clapped his hands gleefully when they took him to the court of justice and stood him in front of the judges. He heard Reuel plead on his behalf, but he did not understand it.

"I say he is but a babe and does things without meaning," Reuel exclaimed. "Put him to the test, and see if he knows the difference between fire and gold. Place before him a dish of fire and a dish of jewels and gold. If he grasps the jewels, it will prove that he is no ordinary child; if he places his hand to the fire, then shall we be assured he is merely a foolish babe."

"So be it," said Bilam, "and if he grasps the jewels let his punishment be instant death."

Pharaoh and the judges agreed, and two dishes, one containing burning coals and the other gold and precious stones were brought in and placed before Moses. Everybody looked on keenly as Moses stared at the dishes. Princess Bathia made signs to him, but Bilam ordered her to cease and it was Reuel who comforted her and dried her tears.

"Take my magic staff," he said, handing to her a stick that seemed to be made of one large precious stone. "This was given to Adam when he left the Garden of Eden and has been handed down to me through Enoch and Noah, through Abraham and Jacob unto Joseph who left it in my keeping. Take the staff and Moses will obey whatsoever be thy wish."

The princess took the staff and pressed it to her lips.

"I wish," she said, "that my little water-babe shall seize the burning coals."

Moses thrust his fingers into the fire and pulled out a glowing coal. With a cry, he put his fingers in his mouth to ease the pain and burned his tongue with the coal. Ever afterward he lisped.

The princess snatched Moses and pressed him tightly to her bosom.

"Give me the magic stick," she said to Reuel, "so that I may guard and protect the child."

"Canst thou read this word?" asked Reuel, pointing to a word engraved on the staff.

"No," said the princess.

"Then it cannot be thine," answered Reuel. "Whosoever reads this name can understand all things, even the thoughts of animals and birds. Fear not for Moses. In years to come this staff shall be his."

And so it came to pass. Years afterward, when Moses was a man and fled from Egypt, he married a daughter of Reuel who became a Hebrew and took the name of Jethro. Reuel planted the staff in his garden and Moses saw it. He read the magic word, and touching the staff it came out of the ground into his hands. With this staff Moses performed the wonderful things in Egypt when he delivered the children of Israel from bondage, as is related in the Bible.

SINBAD OF THE TALMUD

"*R*abba, Rabba, silly, silly Rabba, have you caught another whale to-day?"

With this strange cry a number of children followed an elderly man through the streets of a town in the East. Their parents looked on in amusement and some of them called after the man as the little ones did. Rabba, however, took no notice, but walked straight on with a faraway look in his eyes, as if his thoughts were elsewhere. Presently, on turning the corner of a street, he nearly ran into an Arab coming in the opposite direction. As soon as the children saw the Arab they turned and fled.

"Ali Rabba is coming," they cried to one another in warning, and as fast as their legs would carry them they made off to their homes.

The Arab shook his fist threateningly after the children. Then he turned to the man whom they had followed.

"It is a shame," he said, hotly, "that the impudent ragamuffins of the town should be allowed to cast words of disrespect in the public streets at my sainted master, Rabba bar Chana, the man of profound learning and the famous traveller--"

"Be gentle, good Ali," interrupted Rabba. "Remember they are little more than babes and have not full understanding. And how can they be respectful when their parents, who should have wisdom and faith, accept not our stories of the many adventures we have had? Yesterday, I told them of the day when our ship had been surrounded by five thousand whales, each a mile long, and they jeered and cried 'Impossible!'"

"Impossible!" echoed Ali, in a rage. "Was I not there with thee, my master? Did I not count every single whale myself? Who dares to doubt my word? Have I not, for years, been thy faithful guide on thy marvelous journeys? Bah! What know these town fools, whose lives are no wider than the narrow streets in which they dwell, of the wonders of the vast world beyond the seas? Fools, ignorant fools, every one of them, my good master. Why stay you here with them and brook their insults and their sneers? Let us journey forth again this very day. A good ship waits in the harbor."

Ali's voice grew louder as his rage became stronger and a crowd was collecting. Rabba hurried him away and together they made for the harbor. There they were soon engaged in earnest conversation with the captain of a vessel that had come from a distant land.

"I shall be glad to have two such famous travelers on my ship," said the captain. "I have heard of your adventures, and in my country 'tis said that only those meet with wonders who dare to seek them and believe in them. I, too, would see the wonders of the world, and gladly will I give you passage on my ship."

Next day Rabba and Ali stood on the deck of the vessel as the sail was hoisted, and it moved slowly from the harbor to the accompaniment of cheering and some laughter from a crowd on shore.

"Silly Rabba and Ali Rabba, don't forget to bring back the moon," they cried. "Find out where it goes when it is not here."

Soon the land was out of sight, and scudding before favorable breezes the ship made good progress. In ten days it had reached a sea in which no vessel had ever sailed before. Ali said he could tell this because the fishes behaved queerly. They poked their heads out of the water to gaze at the ship and then darted swiftly out of sight again. It was quite plain that they had never before seen a ship, and they evidently mistook it for some strange sea monster. Every day the fishes grew larger, but no land was sighted until another five days had passed. Then a desert island appeared straight ahead, and the captain steered toward it. A few blades of grass grew here and there, and Rabba determined to land and explore the island.

Accompanied by his faithful Ali, he entered a small boat and was rowed to the shore. They found a few vegetables growing that they had never seen before, and so, collecting twigs from the short, stumpy bushes, they made a fire to cook them. While the vegetables were cooking they looked around.

"It seems a vast land," said Rabba, "and yet over there, about three or four miles away, I think I see water."

"I think so, too," said Ali. "This must be the width of the land, but in the other directions I can see no end. But hark! What sound is that?"

"'Tis like the rumbling of an earthquake," said Rabba, "and I am sure I felt the ground move. Indeed, it seems to me as if it is heaving up and down, like a living thing."

A shout from the boat caused them to look in that direction, and they saw their comrades pointing wildly and calling upon them to come back. Looking in the direction indicated, they saw the land rise up like a huge mountain and a tremendous stream of water gush forth.

"This is not land; this is a whale," cried Rabba, in alarm. "Our fire has wakened it from slumber. Let us hasten to the ship before the monster plunges and drowns us."

They hurried back to the boat and boarded the ship just as the whale began to move. It sank below the waves to quench the fire on its back, but it rose again, and then the vessel found itself in a new danger. It was lying between the body of the monster and one of its fins.

"Let me take command," said Ali. "I know best how to act in times of danger like this. We must avoid being struck by the fin, or we shall be destroyed. We must find which way the monster is moving and go in the opposite direction; otherwise we shall be wrecked when we come to the place where the fin joins the body."

There was no sleep for the crew that night. Everyone watched carefully, for the least false move may have meant instant disaster. Luckily the whale began to move on the surface of the sea against the wind, so that the ship, traveling in the opposite direction, had the wind behind it. Swiftly flew the ship before the breeze, but the fin seemed to have no end, although the whale was traveling fast, too. Three days and three nights the ship continued before it came to the end of the fin. Then everyone on board breathed more freely.

"That was a lucky escape," said the captain to Rabba.

"Speak not too soon," replied the latter. "I have fears yet. We must hasten to get completely away from this monster, but the wind does not favor any alteration of our course."

Even as he spoke there was a great commotion in the water, and the whale began to move back-ward at so fearful a speed that they could scarcely see it. The water was violently agitated and the ship was tossed about as if it were a mere cork. A whole day this lasted. Then the motion grew slower as the head of the whale came past the ship.

"See," cried Ali, excitedly. "A small fish has stuck in the nostril of the monster. That is the cause of this commotion. The monster will surely be killed."

The agitation of the water now died down, and it was seen that the whale was beginning to turn over.

"The monster is dead," said Rabba. "It will float on the waves like a vast desert land and will be a danger to ships."

For several days the vessel was compelled to follow the dead whale. Whenever an attempt was made to move away, the current or the wind changed and the carcass of the monster followed the ship. The captain did not like this at all, for it was dangerous in the extreme. He was afraid that the dead whale would strike the vessel and wreck it.

At last land was sighted. Not even Rabba and Ali could recognize the country. They said they had never seen it before. Beautiful cities dotted the shore, but to everybody's alarm, the body of the whale began to float toward the land.

To make matters worse, a storm arose, and the monster rose and fell with each motion of the angry waves.

"The cities will be destroyed if the whale strikes them," cried Rabba, "and it is impossible for us to warn the people."

Nearer and nearer the whale was driven, while the captain of the ship did his utmost to keep away so as not to be struck by the backwash.

At length, with a tremendous crash, the monster was flung by the waves, which had increased to a great height, against the shore. Above the shrieking of the wind could be heard the noise of falling buildings and the wild cries of the people. A huge wave caught the ship and carried it a mile out to sea and then whirled it back again at a speed that made the crew hold their breath in awe.

It seemed certain that the vessel would be dashed to pieces on the land, and the crew, with cries of warning and alarm, made haste to lash themselves to the masts. The mighty wave swept over the land, over the ruins of the towns, carrying the ship with it, and finally deposited it among the trees of a dense forest a mile from the shore.

"At least we are safe for the present," said Rabba, when he had recovered from the shock and the surprise. "We are more fortunate than the poor people who have been overwhelmed by this strange disaster."

"I should like to know how I am going to get my ship back to the sea," said the captain. "I never heard of such a predicament before."

Rabba merely shrugged his shoulders, and with Ali he walked to the shore. An extraordinary sight met their gaze. Thousands of people were rushing madly to the forests. Everywhere was ruin and desolation. All the towns along the coast, sixty in number they learned afterward, had been destroyed by the stranding of the monster and the tidal wave that followed, and what had not been leveled and swept out to sea had been carried inland to the forests and beyond. All along the coast, as far as the eye could see, lay the body of the whale like a mountain range, and hundreds of people ran up and down, weeping bitterly and wringing their hands.

Rabba gathered as many of them as he could together and addressed them.

"Good people," he said, "ye are the victims of a terrible calamity that has robbed you at one cruel blow of your homes, and many of you of your families. But ye that have survived have duties to yourselves and to the future. In this hour of grief, despair not. There lies the fearful monster that has been your destruction. It shall also be your salvation. Its body can supply you all with food. What you cannot eat, you can salt and store for the future. Thousands of casks of oil can be obtained from its blubber, and with this ye can trade. Then, too, its bones are valuable."

The people thanked Rabba for his good advice, and immediately they set about doing what he bade them. They told him this was a bewitched land, the country of Kishef, abounding with terrible monsters both on land and in the sea, and ruled over by a malignant jinn, named Hormuz, who gave them no peace. They asked Rabba to try and kill this sprite who said that only a stranger to the land could do him harm, and so Rabba and his faithful Ali, mounted on horses, set forth on their adventures.

"I think I know this country," said Ali. "I believe I landed once on the other shore. We cannot be far from the wilderness in which the Israelites wandered."

For several days they journeyed through forests and across plains and nothing happened. At last they came to a broad, high wall which barred their progress. They could find no opening through which to pass, and while they were wondering what to do, a strange figure suddenly appeared on the wall. One of his legs was longer than the other, and his arms were also of different length. His ears and eyes were also unequal, and he hopped and bounded along the wall at amazing speed.

"My name is Hormuz," he cried. "Who are ye?" "Strangers," called Rabba, and as soon as he heard the word, the sprite darted swiftly off along the top of the wall. But although the horses ran at topmost speed, they could not over-take him, and he quickly disappeared. Where he was lost to sight, however, there was a hole in the wall, and through this Rabba and Ali just managed to take their horses. A vast wilderness lay before them.

Ali picked up two clods of earth and smelt them.

"As I thought," he said, "this is the wilderness of the Israelites. Come, I will show thee strange sights."

Before nightfall, they came to a place where the bodies of a large number of men lay strewn on the ground.

"These men must have been giants," said Rabba, as Ali, with his spear uplifted, rode under the raised knee of one of the bodies. "These must be the bodies of the Ephraimites who left Egypt before the rest of the children of Israel and were slain."

He cut off a portion of a garment that still covered one of the bodies, but when he tried to move he could not. He seemed to be rooted to the spot. Nor could his horse move.

"Oh, oh," cried Ali, "my horse has lost its power to move. Thou must have taken something from the dead. Return it, good master, or we shall be held fast here until we perish."

Rabba returned the piece of garment, and they were able to move again. They hurried from the place and came to a chasm in the ground from which smoke was rising.

"This is the pit in which Korah and his children were swallowed," said Ali.

"That must have been a wonderful sight," said Rabba. "I have heard that the pit became like a funnel and that the air all about eddied and sucked in everything that belonged to Korah. Even the things that people had borrowed from him, such as dishes, rolled along the ground from a distance and into the pit. Come, let us hasten away.

They continued their journey for many days, but could not see the demon again. One day the desert ended and they came to the sea. They encamped for the night, and when morning broke Rabba was surprised to find that the basket, in which they kept their provisions, had disappeared.

"I think I can explain," said Ali. "No thieves have been here, but this is the end of the world, the edge of the earth. Here, once in every twenty-four hours, the sky and the earth in their revolution, scrape together. The sky must have caught up your basket and carried it away. It will be returned at the same hour tomorrow morning."

Rabba awoke next morning before the sunrise and saw his basket floating down to earth on a cloud. Both he and All were overjoyed when they recovered it, for they were very hungry. While they were eating, the sky grew dark, and looking up they saw what appeared to be a great cloud above their heads. Out of the sea a mighty tree seemed suddenly to have grown. They moved cautiously forward to investigate.

"Take heed," cried a voice of thunder. "I am a bird standing in the water. It is so deep, with such swift currents, that seven years ago an axe fell in and has not yet reached the bottom."

Rabba and Ali crouched on the ground in great fear, until at last Rabba called: "Mighty bird, we seek your help. We are anxious to find the wicked jinn, Hormuz, and slay him so that people shall be free."

"Follow me," answered the bird, and like a spreading cloud it flew along the coast. Rabba and Ali followed on their horses.

"Look," cried Ali, suddenly, pointing out to sea.

A huge snake and dragon were fighting, and at last the sea-serpent, which was almost as big as the whale that had destroyed the towns, swallowed the dragon. No sooner had it done so, however, than the giant bird swooped down and gobbled up the snake.

"That was a good fat worm for breakfast," called the bird. "Now I shall rest."

It flew toward a gigantic tree which now appeared. So tall was it that its upper branches were lost in the clouds. The bird perched on a branch of the tree.

"Proceed along the coast until you come to two bridges," said the bird. "There you will find Hormuz. Give him two cups of wine to drink, then you can slay him. But be sure you take the diamond from his cap. I, the ziz, give you this warning."

Rabba thanked the bird for its information, and with Ali continued on his journey. After three days they came to a river crossed by two bridges, and with one foot on each stood Hormuz.

As soon as he saw them he began to run, but Rabba called after him, "We bring thee an offering of good wine," and he promptly returned.

Rabba filled the two cups which he had from a leathern bottle, and Hormuz took a cup in each hand, smacking his lips as he did so.

"See," he said, and he tossed the wine into the air, and the wine from the right hand cup fell into the left hand cup and that from the left hand cup into the right and not a drop was spilt. Then he swallowed them both at one gulp.

Almost immediately he fell down in a stupor, and Rabba stabbed him again and again with his spear. Yet, when he seemed quite dead, he jumped up again.

"The diamond," cried Rabba, excitedly, and Ali snatched it from the cap of Hormuz. Then the demon fell dead.

"We can return now," said Rabba, and they set out at once, taking the body with them. They halted only to take food, and the first time they did so a funny thing happened. Ali had killed an animal and Rabba had caught some fish, and, while these were cooking, Rabba took the jinn's diamond from his pocket and examined it. At once the fish and the animal came to life again, jumped out of the cooking pot and made off.

"This is a magic diamond," said Rabba, "that has the power to bring dead things to life. We must keep it covered when we wish to eat."

They did so, and after long journeying they came in sight of the great wall and at last reached the place from which they had started. They had been away twelve months in all, and the people were heartily glad to see them, especially when they heard that Hormuz had been killed and saw his body. They had worked hard on the carcass of the huge whale and were rebuilding the sixty towns and villages that had been destroyed, with the bones of the monster, using the skin as coverings for their tents.

With the help of the magic diamond, Rabba called the ziz, and it took the ship which had been carried into the forest in its beak and flew with it to the sea. Gathering their old comrades, Rabba and Ali set sail for home.

All the inhabitants stood on shore and cheered as long as the ship was in sight. They were sorry that Rabba was gone, but they felt certain now that Hormuz was dead, that nevermore would they be troubled by monsters which brought them such terrible disasters.

THE OUTCAST PRINCE

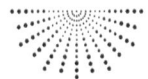

There lived a king who had an only son, on whom he doted. No one, not even his oldest tutor, was permitted to utter a word of correction to the prince whenever he did anything wrong, and so he grew up completely spoiled. He had many faults, but the worst features of his character were that he was proud, arrogant and cruel. Naturally, too, he was selfish and disobedient. When he was called to his lessons, he refused, saying, "I am a prince. Before many years I shall be your king. I have no need to learn what common people must know. Enough for me that I shall occupy the throne and shall rule. My will alone shall prevail. Says not the law of the land, 'The king can do no wrong'?"

Handsome and haughty, even as a youth, he made the king's subjects fear him by his imperious manner. His appearance in the streets was the signal for everyone to run into his house, bar the doors, and peer nervously through the casements. He was a reckless rider, and woe betide the unfortunate persons who happened to be in his way. Sparing neither man, woman, nor child, he callously rode over them, or lashed out vindictively with the long whip he always carried, laughing when anyone screamed with pain.

So outrageous did his public conduct become that the people determined to suffer in silence no longer. They denounced the prince in public, they petitioned the king himself to restrain his son, and his majesty could not disregard the complaints. At first he was merely annoyed, then he was indignant, but when he saw that the people were thoroughly aroused and threatened revolt, he deemed it wise to inquire into the charges against his son.

A commission of three judges was appointed to investigate. They made fullest inquiry and finally laid a document before the king summarizing what they did not hesitate to declare the "infamous actions of His Royal Highness, the Crown Prince."

The king's sense of justice and righteousness at once overcame his foolish pride.

"My people stand justified in their attitude which at first I thought only disrespectful to my royal person," he said. "I owe them an apology and recompense. I shall atone. And my son shall atone, too. He shall not escape punishment."

He summoned his son to appear before him, and the prince entered the royal justice chamber with the air of a braggart, smiling contemptuously at the learned judges who were seated to right and left of his majesty, and defiantly cracking his whip.

"Knowest thou why thou hast been bidden to stand before the judges of the land?" asked the king.

"I know not and I care not," was the haughty answer. "The foolish chatter of the mob interests me not."

The king frowned. He had not seen the prince behave in this fashion before. In the presence of his father, he had always been respectful.

"Thou hast disgraced thy honored name and thy mother's sacred memory, foolish prince," exclaimed the monarch angrily. "Thou hast humiliated thyself and me before the people."

Still the prince tried to laugh off the matter as a joke, but he quickly discovered that the king was in no mood for trifling. Standing grave and erect, his majesty pronounced sentence in a loud and firm voice.

"Know all men," he said, while all the judges, counselors, officers of state and representatives of the people stood awed to silence, "that it having been proved on indisputable evidence that the prince, my son, hath grievously transgressed against the righteous laws of this land and against the people, my subjects, on whom he hath heaped insult, I have taken counsel with my advisers, the ministers of state, and it is my royal will and pleasure to pronounce sentence. Wherefore, I declare that my son, the prince, shall be cast forth into the world, penniless, and shall not return until he shall have learned how to Count Five. And be it further known that none may minister unto his wants should he crave assistance by declaring he is my son, the prince."

The prince stood astounded. What did the mysterious sentence mean?

None could tell him. The only answer to his inquiries was a shrug of the shoulders, for nobody would speak to him.

In the dead of night, with only the stars gazing down on the strange scene, the prince, clad in the cast-off garments of a common laborer, with his golden curls cut off and not a solitary coin in his pocket, was conducted outside the palace grounds and left alone in the road.

He was too much dazed to weep. He told himself this was some horrible dream from which he would waken in the morning, to find himself in his own beautiful room, lying on his gilded bed under the richly embroidered silken coverlet.

When dawn broke, however, he found himself hungry, tired, and his body painfully stiff, under a hedge. He knew now it was no dream but a reality. He was alone and friendless, with no means of earning his food. He understood then what hardships the poor were compelled to undergo, and he began to realize how he had made them suffer, and how, in turn, he was now to pay a heavy price for his brutal treatment of the people.

All that day he wandered aimlessly, until, footsore and exhausted, he sank down at the door of a wayside cottage and begged for food and shelter. These were given to him, and next day he was set to work in the fields. But his hands were not used to labor, and he was sent adrift, his fellow workers jeering at him. With a heavy heart, and his pride humbled, he set forth again to learn the mystery of how to Count Five.

Long days and endless nights, through the heat of the summer, through the snows of winter, the autumnal rains and cold blasts of early spring, he wandered.

A whole year passed away, and he had learned nothing. In truth, he had almost forgotten why he was aimlessly drifting from place to place, farther and farther from his home.

Hunger and thirst were more often than not his daily portion, and the cold earth by night was frequently his couch. Time seemed to drag along without meaning, and oft-times for a week he heard not the sound of a human voice.

He was a beggar, generally accepting gratefully what was given to him, sometimes with harsh words, often with kindly expressions. When he could, he worked, doing anything for small coins, for a rabbi, who had taken compassion on him, had said, "Do any honest work, however repugnant it may at first seem, rather than say haughtily, 'I am the son of a rich father.'"

For a moment he wondered whether the rabbi had guessed his secret, but the learned man said to him he was but repeating a maxim from the Talmud.

Exactly a year from the date of his sentence, as well as he could keep count, the prince found himself in a strange land on the outskirts of a great city. There he fell in with a beggar who hailed him as a brother.

"Come with me," said the beggar. "I know the lore of our fraternity as few do. I know where to obtain the best food and shelter for naught. Here, in this city, a beautiful and noble princess has established a place where all wayfarers may rest and refresh. None are turned away. I will take you thither."

The beggar was as good as his word, and the prince enjoyed the best meal and the most comfortable shelter since he had been an outcast. Overcome with emotion at the thoughts which were conjured up, he retired into a corner and wept. Suddenly he heard a voice of entrancing sweetness say, "Why do you weep?"

He looked up and beheld the most beautiful woman his eyes had ever seen. Instinctively, he rose and bowed low, but made no answer.

"The princess speaks. It is your duty to answer," said another voice, that of an attendant.

A princess! Of course, none but a princess could be so fair. And what a sympathetic voice she possessed. As a prince, he remembered, he had spoken harshly as a rule, and had never visited any of the charitable institutions.

"You must have a history," said the princess, kindly. "Tell it to me. If it is to be kept a secret, you may place confidence in me. I shall not betray you."

The prince was on the point of telling her everything but he hesitated and said:

"Alas! I am an unhappy, wandering beggar, as you see, O most gracious princess. But pity me not. I am not worthy of your kind thoughts. A year ago I dwelt in a--a beautiful house. I was the only son of a--rich merchant, and my father lavished all his love and wealth on me. But I was wicked. I was unkind to people, and I was cast forth and ordered not to return until I had learned to Count Five. I have not yet learned. I am doomed to a wretched life. That is the whole of my history."

"Strange," murmured the princess. "I will help thee if I can."

Next day she came again to the shelter, and with her was the rabbi who had given the prince good counsel. The rabbi made no sign that he had seen the stranger before.

"This sage of the Jews is a wise man and will teach thee," said the princess, and, at her bidding, the prince repeated what he had said the previous night.

"It is a simple lesson," said the rabbi, "so absurdly simple, unfortunately, that proud people overlook it. Tell me, my son," he added. "Vast thou experienced hunger?"

"That I have," returned the prince, sadly.

"Then canst thou count One. Dost thou know what it is to feel cold?"

"I do."

"Two canst thou count. Tell me, further, dost thou know what kindness of heart is?"

"That have I received from the poorest and also from the gracious princess."

"Thou hast proceeded far in thy lesson," said the rabbi. "Thou canst now count Three. Hast thou ever felt gratitude?"

"Indeed I have, often during this past year, and now most particularly."

"Four is now the toll of thy count," said the rabbi. "Tell me, my son, hast thou learned the greatest lesson of all? Dost thou feel humble in spirit?"

With tears in his eyes, the prince answered, "I do, most sincerely."

"Then hast thou truly learned to Count Five. Return to thy father. He must be a wise and just man to impose on thee this lesson. He will assuredly forgive thee. Go, with my blessing," and the rabbi raised his hands above the young man's head and uttered a benediction.

"Take also my good wishes," said the princess, and she offered him her hand to kiss.

"Gracious princess," he said, "it is not meet that a beggar in rags should speak what is in his heart. But I shall return, and if thou deemest me worthy, perchance thou wilt grant a request that I shall make."

"Perchance," replied the princess, with a laugh.

The prince made haste to return to his father's palace and related all his adventures. The old man listened quietly, then he clasped his son in his arms, forgave him, and proudly proclaimed him prince before all the people again. He was a changed man, and nevermore guilty of a cruel action.

Before many months had passed, he returned to the city where he had seen the princess, with a long retinue of attendants, all bearing presents.

"Gracious princess," he said, when he had been granted an audience. "I said I would return."

"Indeed! I know thee not."

The prince told her of their former meeting and she seemed highly pleased.

"Now," he said, "put the crown on thy work which restored to me the manhood I had foolishly cast away by my conduct. I would make thee my bride, and with thee ever my guide and counselor, I shall be the most faithful of kings, and thou a queen of goodness and beauty and wisdom such as the world has not yet seen."

The princess did not give her answer immediately, but in due course she did; and once again, the prince returned home, this time happier than ever. Sitting by his side in the chariot of state, was the princess, radiant in smiles, for the people welcomed her heartily, strewing flowers in her path. And ever afterward there was happiness throughout the land.

THE STORY OF BOSTANAI

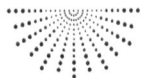

In the days of long ago, when Persia was a famous and beautiful land, with innumerable rose gardens that perfumed the whole country and gorgeous palaces, there lived a king, named Hormuz. He was a cruel monarch, this Shah of Persia. He tyrannized over his people and never allowed them to live in peace. Above all, he hated the Jews.

"These descendants of Abraham," he said to his grand vizier, "never know when they are beaten. How many times it has been reported to me that they have been wiped out of existence, or driven from the land, I know not. Yet nothing, it seems, can crush their spirit. Tell me, why is this?"

"It is because they have a firm faith in their future," answered the vizier.

"What mean you by those words?" demanded the king, angrily.

"I speak only of what I have heard from their wise men," the vizier replied, hastily. "They hold the belief that they will be restored as a united people to their own land."

"Under their own king?" interrupted Hormuz. "Under a descendant of the royal House of David," the vizier answered, solemnly.

The king stamped his foot with rage.

"How dare they think of any other Shah but me," he exclaimed, for his one idea of ruling over people was that he had every right to be cruel to them. Then he said suddenly, "Think you that if there were no more people who could trace their ancestry to this--this David, their faith would be shattered?"

"Peradventure, it may be so."

"It shall be so," cried the king. "There shall be no remnants of this House of David."

He summoned his executioners, and when they were lined up before him, he surveyed the evil-looking band with a cunning gleam in his eye.

"Unto you," he said, in a rasping voice, "I hand over all the descendants of the House of David to be found among the Jews in the whole of the realm of Persia. Slay them instantly. See to it that not a single one--man, woman, or child--is left alive. Woe betide you, and you my counselors"--this with a meaning glance at the grand vizier--"if my commands are not carried out to the letter. To your duties. Ye are dismissed from the presence."

Waving them away, he indulged his fancy in thoughts of the coming executions, chuckling the while.

From day to day he received reports that his commands were being carried out. The land was filled with weeping, for the cruel butchery was worse than war. None could defend themselves. Mere suspicion was enough for the executioners. They wasted no time with doubts, but slew all who were said to belong to the House of David. The Shah looked over the list each night and chuckled. At last he was informed that all had been slaughtered.

"'Tis well, 'tis well," he said, rubbing his hands, gleefully, "I shall sleep in peace tonight."

He slept in a bower in a rose garden, and nowhere in the world are the roses so magnificent and so sweet-scented as in Persia.

"I shall have pleasant dreams," he muttered, but instead he had a nightmare that frightened him terribly.

He dreamed that he was walking in his rose garden, but instead of deriving pleasure from the beautiful trees, he was only angered.

"Are there no white, or yellow, or pink roses?" he asked, but received no answer. "All red, deep, deep red," he muttered, in his troubled manner.

"Tell me," he demanded fiercely, stopping before a tree heavily laden with flowers, "why are you so red today?"

And the roses spoke and replied, "Because of the innocent blood that has been shed. It is royal blood that has drenched the ground, and none but crimson roses shall bloom this year in Persia."

"Bah!" screamed the enraged Shah and, drawing his scimitar, he began hacking right and left among the flowers. The beautiful blooms fell to the ground in great showers until the garden was so littered with the red petals that it seemed flooded with a pool of blood. At last only one tree remained, and as the Shah raised his sword to cut it down, an old man stepped from behind it and confronted the king.

"Who art thou, and whence camest thou?" the monarch asked fiercely.

No answer did the old man make. Gazing sternly into the eyes of the Shah, he raised his hand suddenly and unexpectedly, and struck the king such a violent blow that he fell sprawling to the ground. He lay half-stunned among the red petals, looking up at the old man.

"Art thou not satisfied with the destruction thou hast wrought?" the old man asked. "Must thou take the life of the last rose tree?"

The old man stooped to pick up the scimitar which had fallen from the king's grasp.

"No, no," screamed Hormuz, fearing that he was to be slain. He scrambled to his knees and with clasped hands pleaded to the old man. "Take not my life," he begged. "Spare me, and I shall spare the last tree and cherish it tenderly."

"So be it," said the old man, holding the sword above his head. It dropped to the ground, and looking up, Hormuz saw that the stranger had vanished.

The Shah awoke. His body trembled with fear, his head was wracked by a burning pain. He looked round shudderingly to see if the angry old man still stood above him with the threatening sword. Then he sent for his wizards.

"Expound to me my horrid dream," he said.

Their interpretations, however, did not please him.

"Ye are fools," he cried. "Make search and find me a man of wisdom who understands these mysteries. Seek a sage among the Jews."

The royal servants hastened to do the king's bidding. Full well they knew that when Hormuz was in a rage, lives were quickly forfeit.

They seized the aged rabbi of the city and brought him before the Shah.

"Canst thou interpret dreams?" asked the king, abruptly, dispensing with the usual ceremonies.

"I can explain the meaning of certain things," returned the rabbi.

"Then fail not to unravel the mystery of my dream," said Hormuz, and he related it. "The secret I must know," he concluded, "or-------." But he stopped. He was afraid to add the usual threat of death that morning.

"'Tis a simple dream," said the rabbi, slowly. "The things of which men--and even kings are but men--dream in their sleep are connected with the deeds performed by day. Thy garden represents the House of David which thou hast sought to destroy. The old man was King David himself, and thou hast promised to cherish and nurture his one remaining descendant."

The Shah listened in silence. Then, with a flash in his eye he said, "But all the descendants of this King David were slain."

"All but one," said the rabbi. "There is a boy babe, born on the day the executions ceased."

"Where is he?" asked Hormuz.

"Your vow . . ." the rabbi began, nervously, for he did not wish to hand over this child to death.

"My promise shall be faithfully carried out," interrupted the monarch.

"The boy is in my house," said the rabbi. "His mother, who escaped the massacre, died when he was born."

"Bring him hither," commanded Hormuz. "Fear not."

From his finger he drew a ring and handed it to the learned man.

"This is my bond," he said. "The possession of this ensures thy safety."

The child was brought to the palace, and the Shah looked at him with intent gaze.

"He shall be brought up as a prince," said the king. "Servants, attendants and slaves shall he have in great number to minister unto all his needs. He shall be treated with the utmost kindness. And because of my dream in the garden, I name him Bostanai."

The Shah did this because "bostan" is the Persian word for rose garden.

He touched the child with his jeweled scepter and all present bowed low before the babe and showed him the respect and devotion due to a prince.

Hormuz, however, was too cruel to be quite satisfied. He feared to harm the boy, but he wanted some proof that Bostanai was really a descendant of King David. The child grew up into a handsome, clever youth, and Hormuz, partly out of fear, but partly because he had really grown to love the boy, kept him constantly by his side.

One day, while sitting in the bower in the garden, he watched the boy among the roses. The day was hot and a drowsiness came over the king. He had not slept in that bower since the night of his fateful dream, and he was not happy about doing so now. But he did not lack courage, and he called the boy to him.

"Bostanai," he said, "stand guard by the door, and move not while I sleep."

Hormuz slept soundly and peacefully for some time, and when he awoke he saw the lad standing motionless where he had placed himself.

"Bostanai," he called, and when the boy turned, he was startled to see blood trickling from a wound on his face.

"What is that?" he asked, anxiously.

"The sting of a wasp," Bostanai replied.

"Is it not painful?"

For answer, the boy only smiled.

"How did it happen?" asked the king.

"The wasp stung me while I stood guard."

"But couldst thou not brush it away?"

"No," replied the boy, proudly. "King David was my ancestor, and in the presence of a king I must stand motionless until bidden to make any movement."

Then, before the king could catch him, he swooned from loss of blood, and fell to the ground. He soon recovered, however, and the Shah's doubts were set at rest.

"I know now thou art truly of the House of David," he said, "for none other could have shown such fortitude."

Bostanai became the Shah's favorite, and when he grew up he was made the ruler of a province. He lived happily, and through him the Jews of the land also lived in prosperity and peace.

FROM SHEPHERD-BOY TO KING

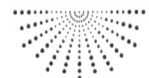

On a desolate plain, a little shepherd-boy stood alone. His day's work was over and he had wandered through field and forest listening to the twittering of the birds and the soft sound of the summer breezes as they gently swayed the branches of the trees. He seemed to understand what the birds were saying, and the murmuring of the brook that wound its way through the forest was like a message of Nature to him. Sweet sounds were always in his ears, his heart was ever singing, for the shepherd-boy was a poet. At times he would turn around sharply, thinking he had heard some one calling. One day he was quite startled.

"David, David," he thought he heard a voice calling, "thou shalt be King of Israel."

But he could see nothing, except the trees and the flowers, and so he left the forest and stood in the desolate plain. In the distance he saw a very high hill and as he approached nearer he noticed on the summit a tall tree, without branches or leaves. With great difficulty he climbed the hill. It was quite smooth, bare of vegetation and without rocks, and little David noticed that it gave forth none of those sweet sounds like music that came from other hills.

The summit gained, he looked at the tree in wonderment. It was not of wood, but of horn.

"'Tis strange," said the boy. "This must be a magic mountain. No tree, or flower, or shrub, can grow in this barren earth."

He tried to dig a clod of earth out of the ground, but could not do so, even with his knife, for the ground was as hard as if covered with tough hide.

David was greatly puzzled, but, being a boy of courage, he did not begin to run down the mountain.

"I wonder what will happen if I stay here," he said, and he seated himself at the foot of the mysterious horn that grew at the summit and looked about him.

Then he noticed a most peculiar thing. The ground was rising and falling in places as if moved by some power beneath. Listening intently, he also heard a curious rumbling noise, and then a loud-sounding swish. At the same time he saw something rising from the other end of the mountain and whirl through the air.

"That is just like a tail," exclaimed David in surprise.

The next minute he had to cling with all his might to the horn, for the whole mountain was moving. It was rising, and soon David was quite near the clouds. The earth was a great distance away, and, judging by a tremendous shadow cast by the sun, David could see that he was clinging to the horn of a gigantic animal.

"I know what it is now," he said. "This is not a mountain, but a unicorn. The monster must have been lying asleep when I mistook it for a hill."

David began to puzzle his brain as to a means of getting down from his perilous perch.

"I must wait," he said, "until the animal feeds. He will surely lower his head to the ground then and I will slip off."

But a new terror awaited him. The roar of a lion was heard in the distance, and David found that he could understand it.

"Bow to me, for I am king of the beasts," the lion roared.

The lion, however, was so small compared with the unicorn that David could scarcely see it. The unicorn, as soon as it heard the command, began to lower its head, and soon David was enabled to slip to the ground. To his alarm he found himself just in front of the lion. The king of the beasts stood before him with blazing eyes, lashing its sides with his tail. David lost not a moment. Drawing his knife from his belt, the brave boy advanced boldly toward the lion.

Just then a sound attracted the attention of both the boy and the beast. It was a deer.

"I will save thee, boy," it cried. "Mount my back and trust to my speed."

Before the lion could recover from its surprise, David had sprung on to the back of the deer which started to run at lightning speed. David clung tightly to its back. Behind him a fierce roar indicated that the lion was in pursuit. Across the desolate plain and through the forest the chase continued, and when David came within sight of human habitations again, the deer stopped.

"Thou art safe now," the deer said to him.

"Thou art to become king, and my command was to save thee. Fear not, I will lead the lion astray." David thanked the deer that had so gallantly saved his life, and as soon as he had slid from its back it dashed off again, faster than ever with the lion still in pursuit. Soon both were out of sight.

David sang light-heartedly as he returned to his humble home and years afterward, when he was king of Israel and remembered his escape, he put the words of his song into one of his Psalms.

THE MAGIC PALACE

Ibrahim, the most learned and pious man of the city, whom everybody held in esteem, fell on troubled days. To none did he speak of his sufferings, for he was proud and would have been compelled to refuse the help which he knew would have been offered to him. His noble wife and five faithful sons suffered in silence, but Ibrahim was sorely troubled when he saw their clothes wearing away to rags and their bodies wasting with hunger.

One day Ibrahim was seated in front of the Holy Book, but he saw not the words on its pages. His eyes were dimmed with tears and his thoughts were far away. He was day-dreaming of a region where hunger and thirst and lack of clothes and shelter were unknown. He sighed heavily and his wife heard.

"My dear husband," she said to him gently, "we are starving. You must go forth to seek work for the sake of our five little sons."

"Yes, yes," he replied, sadly, "and for you, too, my devoted wife, but"-- and he pointed to his tattered garments--"how can I go out in these? Who will employ a man so miserably clad?"

"I will ask our kind neighbors to lend you some raiment," said his wife, and although he made some demur at first, she did so and was successful in obtaining the loan of a cloak which completely covered Ibrahim and restored to him his dignified appearance.

His good wife cheered him with brave words. He took his staff and set out with head erect and his heart filled with a great hope. All people saluted the learned Ibrahim, for it was not often he was seen abroad in the busy streets of the city. He returned their greetings with kindly smiles, but halted not in his walk. He had no wish to make any claims upon his fellow citizens, who would no doubt have gladly assisted him. He desired to go among strangers and work so that he should not be beholden to anyone.

Beyond the city gates, where the palm trees grew and the camels trudged lazily toward the distant desert, he was suddenly accosted by a stranger dressed as an Arab.

"O learned and holy man of the city," he said, "command me, for I am thy slave." At the same time he made a low bow before Ibrahim.

"My slave!" returned Ibrahim, in surprise. "You mock me, stranger. I am wretchedly poor. I seek but the opportunity to sell myself, even as a slave, to any man who will provide food and clothing for my wife and children."

"Sell not thyself," said the Arab. "Offer me for sale instead. I am a marvelous builder. Behold these plans and models, specimens of my skill and handiwork."

From beneath the folds of his ample robes, the Arab produced a scroll and a box and held them out to Ibrahim. The latter took them, wonderingly. On the scroll were traced designs of stately buildings. Within the box was an exquisite model of a palace, a marvelous piece of work, perfect in detail and workmanship. Ibrahim examined it with great care.

"I have never seen anything so beautiful," he admitted. "It is wrought and fashioned with exceeding good taste. It is in itself a work of art. You must indeed be a wondrous craftsman. Whence come you?"

"What matters that?" replied the Arab. "I am thy slave. Is there not in this city some rich merchant or nobleman who needs the services of such talents as I possess? Seek him out and dispose of me to him. To thee he will give ear; to me he will not listen."

Ibrahim pondered over this strange request for a while.

"Agreed!" he said, at length.

Together they returned to the city. There Ibrahim made inquiries in the bazaar where the wealthy traders met to discuss their affairs, and soon learned of a rich dealer in precious stones, a man of a multitude of charitable deeds, who was anxious to erect an imposing residence. He called upon the jeweler.

"Noble sir," he said, "I hear that it is thy intention to erect a palace the like of which this city has not yet seen, an edifice that will be an everlasting joy to its possessor, a delight to all who gaze upon it, and which will bring renown to this city."

"That is so," said the merchant. "You have interpreted the desire of my heart as if you had read its secret. I would fain dedicate to the uses of the ruler of this city a palace that will shed luster on his name."

"It is well," returned Ibrahim. "I have brought thee an architect and builder of genius. Examine his plans and designs. If they please thee, as assuredly they will, purchase the man from me, for he is my slave."

The jeweler could not understand the plans on the scroll, but on the model in the box he feasted his eyes for several minutes in speechless amazement.

"It is indeed remarkable," he said at last. "I will give thee eighty thousand gold pieces for thy slave, who must build for me just such a palace."

Ibrahim immediately informed the Arab, who at once consented to perform the task, and then the pious man hastened home to his wife and children with the good news and the money, which made him rich for the rest of his days.

To the Arab the jeweler said, "Thou wilt regain thy liberty if thou wilt succeed in thy under-taking. Begin at once. I will forthwith engage the workmen."

"I need no workmen," was the Arab's singular reply. "Take me to the land whereon I must build, and to-morrow thy palace shall be complete."

"Tomorrow!"

"Even as I say," answered the Arab.

The sun was setting in golden glory when they reached the ground, and pointing to the sky the Arab said: "Tomorrow, when the great orb of light rises above the distant hills, its rays will strike the minarets and domes and towers of thy palace, noble sir. Leave me now. I must pray."

In perfect bewilderment, the merchant left the stranger. From a distance he watched the man devoutly praying. He had made up his mind to watch all the night; but when the moon rose, deep sleep overcame him and he dreamed. He dreamed that he saw myriads of men swarming about strange machines and scaffolding which grew higher and higher, hiding a vast structure.

Ibrahim dreamed, too, but in his vision one figure, that of the Arab, stood out above all other things. Ibrahim scanned the features of the stranger closely; he followed, as it were, the man's every movement. He noticed how all the workmen and particularly the supervisors did the stranger great honor, showing him the deference due to one of the highest position. And with grave and dignified mien, the Arab responded kindly. From the heavens a bright light shone upon the scene, the radiance being softest wherever the Arab stood.

THE MAGIC PALACE | 89

In his dream, it so appeared to Ibrahim, he rose from his bed, went out into the night, and approached the palace magically rising from the waste ground beyond the city. Nearer and nearer his footsteps took him, until he stood beside the Arab again. One of the chief workmen approached and addressed the stranger--by name!

Then it was Ibrahim understood--and he awoke. The sun was streaming in through the lattice of his bedroom. He sprang from his bed and looked out upon a magnificent spectacle. Beyond the city the sun's rays were reflected by a dazzling array of gilded cupolas and glittering spires, the towers of the palace of marble that he had seen builded in his dream. Instantly he went out and made haste to the palace to assure himself that his dream was really over. Ibrahim and the jeweler arrived before the gates at the same moment. They stood speechless with amazement and admiration before the model of the Arab grown to immense proportions.

Almost at the same moment, the gates, ornamented with beaten gold, opened from within and the Arab stood before them. Ibrahim bent low his head.

The Arab addressed the merchant.

"Have I fulfilled my promise and earned my freedom?" he asked.

"Verily thou hast," answered the merchant.

"Then farewell, and may blessings rest on thee and the good Ibrahim and on all your works."

Thus spoke the Arab, raising his hands in benediction. Then he disappeared within the golden doors.

The jeweler and Ibrahim followed quickly, but though they hastened through the halls and corridors of many colored marbles, in and out of rooms lighted by windows of clearest crystal, and up and down staircases of burnished metal, they could find no one. Emerging into the open again, they saw a huge crowd standing in wonderment before the gates.

"Tell me," said the jeweler, "who was the builder of this magic palace."

"Elijah, the Prophet," said Ibrahim, "the benefactor of mankind, who revisits the earth to assist in their distress those deemed worthy. Blessed am I, and blessed art thou for thy good deeds, for we have been truly honored."

To show his gratitude, the merchant gave a banquet in his palace to all the people in the city and scattered gold and silver pieces among the crowds that thronged the streets.

THE SLEEP OF ONE HUNDRED YEARS

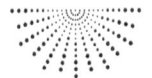

It was at the time of the destruction of the First Temple. The cruel war had laid Jerusalem desolate, and terrible was the suffering of the people.

Rabbi Onias, mounted on a camel, was sorrow-fully making his way toward the unhappy city. He had traveled many days and was weary from lack of sleep and faint with hunger, yet he would not touch the basket of dates he had with him, nor would he drink from the water in a leather bottle attached to the saddle.

"Perchance," he said, "I shall meet some one who needs them more than I."

But everywhere the land was deserted. One day, nearing the end of the journey, he saw a man planting a carob tree at the foot of a hill.

"The Chaldeans," said the man, "have destroyed my beautiful vineyards and all my crops, but I must sow and plant anew, so that the land may live again."

Onias passed sorrowfully on and at the top of the hill he stopped. Before him lay Jerusalem, not the once beautiful city with its hundreds of domes and minarets that caught the first rays of the sun each morning, but a vast heap of ruins and charred buildings. Onias threw himself on the ground and wept bitterly. No human being could he see, and the sun was setting over what looked like a city of the dead.

"Woe, woe," he cried. "Zion, my beautiful Zion, is no more. Can it ever rise again? Not in a hundred years can its glory be renewed."

The sun sank lower as he continued to gaze upon the ruined city, and darkness gathered over the scene. Utterly exhausted, Onias, laying his head upon his camel on the ground, fell into a deep sleep.

The silver moon shone serenely through the night and paled with the dawn, and the sun cast its bright rays on the sleeping rabbi. Darkness spread its mantle of night once more, and again the sun rose, and still Onias slept. Days passed into weeks, the weeks merged into months, and the months rolled on until years went by; but Rabbi Onias did not waken.

Seeds, blown by the winds and brought by the birds, dropped around him, took root and grew into shrubs, and soon a thick hedge surrounded him and screened him from all who passed. A date that had fallen from his basket, took root also, and in time there rose a beautiful palm tree which cast a shade over the sleeping figure.

And thus a hundred years rolled by.

Suddenly, Onias moved, stretched himself and yawned. He was awake again. He looked around confused.

"Strange," he muttered. "Did I not fall asleep on a hill overlooking Jerusalem last night? How comes it now that I am hemmed in by a thicket and am lying in the shade of this noble date palm?"

With great difficulty he rose to his feet.

"Oh, how my bones do ache!" he cried. "I must have overslept myself. And where is my camel?"

Puzzled, he put his hand to his beard. Then he gave a cry of anguish.

"What is this? My beard is snow-white and so long that it almost reaches to the ground."

He sank down again, but the mound on which he sat was but a heap of rubbish and collapsed under his weight. Beneath it were bones. Hastily clearing away the rubbish, he saw the skeleton of a camel.

"This surely must be my camel," he said. "Can I have slept so long? The saddle-bags have rotted, too. But what is this?" and he picked up the basket of dates and the water-bottle. The dates and the water were quite fresh.

"This must be some miracle," he said. "This must be a sign for me to continue my journey. But, alas, that Jerusalem should be destroyed!"

He looked around and was more puzzled than ever. When he had fallen asleep the hill had been bare of vegetation. Now it was covered with carob trees.

"I think I remember a man planting a carob tree yesterday," he said. "But was it yesterday?"

He turned in the other direction and gave a cry of astonishment. The sun was shining on a noble city of glittering pinnacles and minarets, and around it were smiling fields and vineyards.

"Jerusalem still lives," he exclaimed. "Of a truth I have been dreaming--dreaming that it was destroyed. Praise be to God that it was but a dream."

With all speed he made his way across the plain to the city. People looked at him strangely and pointed him out to one another, and the children ran after him and called him names he did not understand. But he took no notice. Near the outskirts of the city he paused.

"Canst thou tell me, father," he said to an old man, "which is the house of Onias, the rabbi?"

"'Tis thy wit, or thy lack of it, that makes thee call me father," replied the man. "I must be but a child compared with thee."

Others gathered around and stared hard at Onias.

"Didst thou speak of Rabbi Onias?" asked one. "I know of one who says that was the name of his grandfather. I will bring him."

He hastened away and soon returned with an aged man of about eighty.

"Who art thou?" Onias asked.

"Onias is my name," was the reply. "I am called so in honor of my sainted grandfather, Rabbi Onias, who disappeared mysteriously one hundred years ago, after the destruction of the First Temple."

"A hundred years," murmured Onias. "Can I have slept so long?"

"By thy appearance, it would seem so," replied the other Onias. "The Temple has been rebuilt since then."

"Then it was not a dream," said the old man.

They led him gently indoors, but everything was strange to him. The customs, the manners, the habits of the people, their dress, their talk, was all different, and every time he spoke they laughed.

"Thou seemest like a creature from another world," they said. "Thou speakest only of the things that have long passed away."

One day he called his grandson.

"Lead me," he said, "to the place of my long sleep. Perchance I will sleep again. I am not of this world, my child. I am alone, a stranger here, and would fain leave ye."

Taking the dates and the bottle of water which still remained fresh, he made his way to where he had slept for a hundred years, and there his prayer for peace was answered. He slept again, but not in this world will he awaken.

KING FOR THREE DAYS

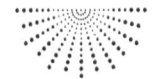

Godfrey de Bouillon was a famous warrior, a daring general and bold leader of men, who gained victories in several countries. And so, in the year 1095, when the first Crusade came to be arranged, he was entrusted with the command of one of the armies and led it across Europe in the historic march to the Holy Land.

Like many a great soldier of his period, Godfrey was a cruel man, and, above all, he hated the Jews.

"In this, our Holy War," he said to his men, "we shall slay all the children of Israel wherever we shall fall in with them. I shall not rest content until I have exterminated the Jews."

True to his inhuman oath, Godfrey and his soldiers massacred large numbers of Jews. They did this without pity or mercy, saying: "We are performing a sacred duty, for we have the blessings of the priests on our enterprise."

Godfrey felt sure he would be victorious, but he also wanted to obtain the blessing of a rabbi. It was a curious desire, but in those days such things were not considered at all strange, and so Godfrey de Bouillon sent for the learned Rabbi Solomon ben Isaac, better known by his world-famed name of Rashi.

Rashi, one of the wisest sages of the Jews, came to Godfrey, and the two men stood facing each other.

"Thou halt heard of my undertaking to capture Jerusalem," said Godfrey, haughtily. "I demand thy blessing on my venture."

"Blessings are not in the gift of man; they are bestowed by Heaven--on worthy objects," answered Rashi.

"Trifle not with words," retorted the warrior, or they may cost thee dear. A holy man can invoke a blessing."

But Rashi was not afraid. He was becoming an old man then, but he was as brave as the swaggering soldier, and he faced Godfrey unflinchingly.

"I can make no claim on the God of Israel on behalf of one who has sworn to destroy all the descendants of His chosen people," he said.

"So, ho!" exclaimed Godfrey, "you defy me.'

But he stopped his angry words abruptly,

He had no wish to quarrel with any holy man, for that might make him nervous. And nervousness, then, was misunderstood as superstition. Besides, the rabbi might curse him.

"If you will not bless," he said, "perhaps you will deign to raise the veil of the future for me. You wise men of the Jews are seers and can foretell events--so they say. A hundred thousand chariots filled with soldiers brave, determined and strong, are at my command. Tell me, shall I succeed, or fail?"

"Thou wilt do both." Rashi replied.

"What mean you?" demanded Godfrey, angrily.

"This. Jerusalem will fall to thee. So it is ordained, and thou wilt become its king."

"Ha, ha! So you deem it wisest to pronounce a blessing after all," interrupted Godfrey. "I am content."

"I have not spoken all," said the rabbi, gravely. "Three days wilt thou rule and no more."

Godfrey turned pale.

"Shall I return?" he asked, slowly.

"Not with thy multitude of chariots. Thy vast army will have dwindled to three horses and three men when thou reachest this city."

"Enough," cried Godfrey. "If you think to affright me with these ominous words, you fail in your intent. And hearken, Rabbi of the Jews, your words shall be remembered. Should they prove incorrect in the minutest detail--if I am King of Jerusalem for four days, or return with four horsemen--you shall pay the penalty of a false prophet and shall be consigned to the flames. Do you understand? You shall be put to death."

"I understand well," returned Rashi, quite unmoved, "it is a sentence which you and your kind love to pronounce with or without the sanction of those whom you call your holy men. It is not I who fear, Godfrey de Bouillon. I seek not to peer into the future to assure my own safety."

With these words they parted, the rabbi returning to his prayers and to his studies which have enriched the learning of the Jews, while Godfrey proceeded to lay a trail of innocent Jewish blood along the banks of the Rhine in his march to Palestine.

History has set on record the events of the Crusade. Godfrey, after many battles, laid siege to the Holy City, captured it, and drove the Jews into one of the synagogues and burned them alive. Eight days afterward, his soldiers raised him on their shields and proclaimed him king.

Godfrey was delighted, but two days later he thought the matter over carefully and decided that he could not live in Jerusalem always. So next day he called together his captains and said:

"You have done me great honor. But I must return to Europe, and it would be more befitting that I should be styled Duke of Jerusalem and Guardian of the Holy City than its sovereign."

That night, however, he suddenly remembered the prediction of Rashi.

"For three days I have been King of Jerusalem," he muttered. "The rabbi of the Jews spoke truth."

He could not help wondering whether the rest of the prophecy would be fulfilled, and he became moody. He was joyful when he gained a victory, but there came also disasters, and he was plunged into despondency. The reverses affected the buoyancy of his troops, disease decimated their ranks, and desertions further depleted their numbers. Slowly but surely his mighty army dwindled away to a mere handful of dissatisfied men and decrepit horses.

It was a ragged and wretched procession that he led back across Europe, and daily his retinue grew smaller. Men and horses dropped from sheer fatigue helpless by the wayside, and were left there to die, with the hungry vultures perched on trees, patiently waiting for the last flicker of life to depart before they set to work to pick the bones of all flesh.

Godfrey de Bouillon had gained his victory, but at what cost? Thousands of men, women and children had been murdered, thousands of his soldiers had fallen in battle, and now hundreds of others had dropped out of the ranks to end their last hours on the ghastly road that led from Jerusalem back to western Europe. Do you wonder that Godfrey was unhappy, and that he thought every moment of the words of Rashi?

At length he reached the city of Worms where Rashi dwelt. With him were four men, mounted on horses.

"It is well," he said, with as much cheerfulness as he could muster, as he surveyed the remnants of his once proud army. "The rabbi has failed."

Godfrey bade his men fall into line behind him and he proudly rode through the gate of the city. As he did so, he heard a cry of alarm. He turned hastily and saw a huge stone falling from the city's gate. It dropped on the soldier riding just behind him, killing both man and horse.

"You have spoken truth; would that I had taken heed of your words," he said to the rabbi. "I am a broken man. You will assuredly achieve great fame in Israel."

And so it has come to pass. Should you, by chance, ever visit the city of Brussels, the capital of Belgium, fail not to look upon the statue of Godfrey de Bouillon, with his sword proudly raised. It stands in the Place Royale but a few minutes' walk from the synagogue. Should you ever be in the ancient city of Worms that stands on the Rhine, do as other visitors, Jews and Gentiles-- enter the synagogue that was built many centuries ago, and you will see the room where Rashi studied and the stone seat on which he sat. And not far from the synagogue you will see the ancient gate of the city, named in honor of Rabbi Solomon ben Isaac, the Rashi Gate. Perhaps it is the very one under which Godfrey de Bouillon passed into the city with his three mounted companions, as the legend tells.

THE PALACE IN THE CLOUDS

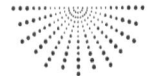

*I*kkor, the Jewish vizier of the king of Assyria, was the wisest man in the land, but he was not happy. He was the greatest favorite of the king who heaped honors upon him, and the idol of the people who bowed before him in the streets and cast themselves on the ground at his feet to kiss the hem of his garment. Always he had a kindly word and a smile for those who sought his advice and guidance, but his eyes were ever sad, and tears would trickle down his cheeks as he watched the little children at play in the streets.

His fame as a man of wisdom was known far beyond the borders of Assyria, and rulers feared to give offense to the king who had Ikkor as the chief of his counselors to assist in the affairs of state. But Ikkor would oft sit alone in his beautiful palace and sigh heavily. No sound of children's laughter was ever heard in the palace of Ikkor, and that was the cause of his sorrow. Ikkor was a pious man and deeply learned in the Holy Law; and he had prayed long and devoutly and had listened unto the advice of magicians that he might be blessed with but one son, or even a daughter, to carry down his name and renown. But the years passed and no child was born to him.

Every year, on the advice of the king, he married another wife, and now he had in his harem thirty wives, all childless. He determined to take unto himself no more wives, and one night he dreamed a dream in which a spirit appeared to him and said:

"Ikkor, thou wilt die full of years and honor, but childless. Therefore, take Nadan, the son of thy widowed sister and let him be a son to thee."

Nadan was a handsome youth of fifteen, and Ikkor related his dream to the boy's mother who permitted him to take Nadan to his palace and there bring him up as his own son. The sadness faded from the vizier's eyes as he watched the lad at his games and his lessons, and Ikkor himself imparted wisdom to Nadan. But, first to his surprise, and then to his grief, Nadan was not thankful for the riches and love lavished upon him. He neglected his lessons and grew proud, haughty and arrogant. He treated the servants of the household harshly and did not obey the wise maxims of Ikkor.

The vizier, however, was hopeful that he would reform and gain wisdom with years, and he took him to the palace of the king and appointed him an officer of the royal guard. For Ikkor's sake, the king made Nadan one of his favorites, and all in the land looked upon the young man as the successor of Ikkor and the future vizier. This only served to make Nadan still more arrogant, and a wicked idea entered his head to gain further favor with the king and supplant Ikkor at once.

"O King, live for ever!" he said one day, when Ikkor was absent in a distant part of the land; "it grieves me to have to utter words of warning against Ikkor, the wise, the father who has adopted me. But he conspires to destroy thee."

The king laughed at this suggestion, but he became serious when Nadan promised to give him proof in three days. Nadan then set to work and wrote two letters. One was addressed to Pharaoh, king of Egypt, and read as follows:

"Pharaoh, son of the Sun and mighty ruler on earth, live for ever! Thou wouldst reign over Assyria. Give ear then to my words and on the tenth day of the next month come with thy troops to the Eagle Plain beyond the city, and I, Ikkor, the grand vizier, will deliver thine enemy, the King of Assyria, into thy hands."

To this letter he forged Ikkor's name; then he took it to the king.

"I have found this," he said, "and have brought it to thee. It shows thee that Ikkor would deliver this country to thine enemy."

The king was very angry and would have sent for Ikkor at once, but Nadan counseled patience.

"Wait until the tenth of next month, the day of the annual review, and thou wilt see what will surprise thee still more," he said.

Then he wrote the second letter. This was to Ikkor and was forged with the king's name and sealed with the king's seal which he obtained. It bade

Ikkor on the tenth of the next month to assemble the troops on the Eagle Plain to show how numerous they were to the foreign envoys and to pretend to attack the king, so as to demonstrate how well they were drilled.

The vizier returned the day before the review, and while the king stood with Nadan and the foreign envoys, Ikkor and the troops, acting on their instructions, made a pretense of attacking his majesty.

"Do you not see?" said Nadan. "The king of Egypt not being here, Ikkor threatens thee," and he immediately gave orders to the royal trumpeters to sound "Halt!"

Ikkor was brought before the king and confronted with the letter to Pharaoh.

"Explain this, if thou canst," exclaimed the king, angrily. "I have trusted thee and loaded thee with riches and honors and thou wouldst betray me. Is not this thy signature, and is not thy seal appended?"

Ikkor was too much astounded to reply, and Nadan whispered to the king that this proved his guilt.

"Lead him to the execution," cried the king, "and let his head be severed from his body and cast one hundred ells away."

Falling on his knees, Ikkor pleaded that at least he should be granted the privilege of being executed within his own house so that he might be buried there.

This request was granted, and Nabu Samak, the executioner, led Ikkor a prisoner to his palace. Nabu Samak was a great friend to Ikkor and it grieved him to have to carry out the king's order.

"Ikkor," he said, "I am certain that thou art innocent, and I would save thee. Hearken unto me. In the prison is a wretched highwayman who has committed murder and who deserves death. His beard and hair are like thine, and at a little distance he can easily be mistaken for thee. Him will I behead and his head will I show to the crowd, whilst thou canst hide and live in secret."

Ikkor thanked his friend and the plan was carried out. The robber's head was exhibited to the crowd from the roof of the house and the people wept because they thought it was the head of the good Ikkor. Meanwhile, the vizier descended into a cellar deep beneath his palace and was there fed, while his adopted son, Nadan, was appointed chief of the king's counselors in his stead.

Now, when Pharaoh, king of Egypt, heard that Ikkor, the wise, had been executed, he determined to make war upon Assyria. Therefore, he dispatched a letter to the king, asking him to send an architect to design and build a palace in the clouds.

"If this thou doest," he wrote, "I, Pharaoh, son of the Sun, will pay thee tribute; if thou failest, thou must pay me tribute."

The king of Assyria was perplexed when he received this letter which had to be answered in three months. Nadan could not advise him what to do, and he bitterly regretted that Ikkor, the man of wisdom, was no longer by his side to advise him.

"I would give one-fourth of my kingdom to bring Ikkor to life again," he exclaimed.

Hearing these words, Nabu Samak, the executioner, fell on his knees and confessed that Ikkor was alive.

"Bring him hither at once," cried the king.

Ikkor could scarcely credit the truth when his friend came to him in the cellar with the news, and the people wept tears of joy and pity when the old vizier was led through the streets. He presented a most extraordinary spectacle.

For twelve months he had been immured in the cellar and his beard had grown down to the ground, his hair descended below his shoulders and his finger nails were several inches long. The king wept, too, when he saw his old vizier.

"Ikkor," he said, "for months have I felt that thou wert innocent, and I have missed thy wise counsels. Help me in my difficulty and thou shalt be pardoned."

"Your majesty," said Ikkor, "I desire nothing more than to serve thee. I am innocent. Time will prove me guiltless."

When he saw Pharaoh's demand, he smiled. "'Tis easy," he said. "I will go to Egypt and outwit Pharaoh."

He gave orders that four of the tame eagles in the gardens of the palace should be brought to him with cords five hundred ells long attached to their claws. Then he selected four youths, lithe of figure, and trained them to sit on the backs of the eagles and soar aloft. This done, he set out for Egypt with a big caravan and a long retinue of slaves.

"What is thy name?" asked Pharaoh, when he presented himself.

"My name is Akbam, and I am but the lowest of my king's advisers."

"Does thy master then think my demand so simple?" asked Pharaoh.

Ikkor bowed to indicate that this was so, and Pharaoh was much annoyed and puzzled.

"Perform thy task and at once," he commanded.

At a sign from Ikkor, the four youths mounted the eagles which flew aloft to the extremity of their cords. The birds remained in the air two hundred ells apart, as they had been trained, and the lads held cords in the form of a square.

"That is the plan of the palace in the clouds," said Ikkor, pointing aloft. "Bid your men carry up bricks and mortar. The task is so simple that the boys will build."

Pharaoh frowned. He had not expected to be thus outwitted, but he would not immediately acknowledge this.

"In this land," he said, sarcastically, "we use no mortar. We sew the stones together. Canst thou do this?"

"Easily," replied Ikkor, "if your wise men can make me a thread of sand."

"And canst thou weave a thread of sand?" asked Pharaoh.

"I can," responded Ikkor.

Noting the direction of the sun, he bored a tiny hole in the wall, and a thin sunbeam gleamed through. Then, taking a few grains of sand he blew them through the hole and in the sunbeam they seemed like a thread.

"Take it, quickly," he cried, but of course nobody could do this.

Pharaoh looked long and earnestly at Ikkor.

"Truly, thou art a man of wisdom," he said. "If he were not dead I should say thou wert Ikkor, the wise."

"I am Ikkor," answered the vizier, and he told the story of his escape.

"I will prove thy innocence," exclaimed Pharaoh. "I will write a letter to your royal master."

Not only did he do so, but he gave Ikkor many valuable presents and the vizier returned to Assyria, resumed his place by the king's side, and became a greater favorite than before. Nadan was banished and was never heard of again.

THE POPE'S GAME OF CHESS

Nearly a thousand years ago in the town of Mayence, on the bank of the Rhine, there dwelt a pious Jew of the name of Simon ben Isaac. Of a most charitable disposition, learned and ever ready to assist the poor with money and wise counsel, he was reverenced by all, and it was believed he was a direct descendant of King David. Everybody was proud to do him honor.

Simon ben Isaac had one little son, a bright boy of the name of Elkanan, who he intended should be trained as a rabbi. Little Elkanan was very diligent in his studies and gave early promise of developing into an exceptionally clever student. Even the servants in the household loved him for his keen intelligence. One of them, indeed, was unduly interested in him.

She was the Sabbath-fire woman who only came into the house on the Sabbath day to attend to the fires, because, as you know, the Jewish servants could not perform this duty. The Sabbath-fire woman was a devoted Catholic and she spoke of Elkanan to a priest. The latter was considerably impressed.

"What a pity," he remarked, "that so talented a boy should be a Jew. If he were a Christian, now," he added, winningly, "he could enter the Holy Church and become famous."

The Sabbath-fire woman knew exactly what the priest meant.

"Do you think he could rise to be a bishop?" she asked.

"He might rise even higher--to be the Pope himself," replied the priest.

"It would be a great thing to give a bishop to the Church, would it not?" said the woman.

"It is a great thing to give anyone to the Church of Rome," the priest assured her.

Then they spoke in whispers. The woman appeared a little troubled, but the priest promised her that all would be well, that she would be rewarded, and that nobody would dare to accuse her of doing anything wrong.

Convinced that she was performing a righteous action, she agreed to do what the priest suggested.

Accordingly, the following Friday night when the household of Simon ben Isaac was wrapped in slumber, she crept stealthily and silently into the boy's bedroom. Taking him gently in her arms, she stole silently out of the house and carried him to the priest who was waiting. Elkanan was well wrapped up in blankets, and so cautiously did the woman move that he did not waken.

The priest said not a word. He just nodded to the woman, and then placed Elkanan in a carriage which he had in waiting.

Elkanan slept peacefully, totally unaware of his adventure, and when he opened his eyes he thought he must be dreaming. He was not in his own room, but a much smaller one which seemed to be jolting and moving, like a carriage, and opposite to him was a priest.

"Where am I?" he asked in alarm.

"Lie still, Andreas," was the reply.

"But my name is not Andreas," he answered. "That is not a Jewish name. I am Elkanan, the son of Simon."

To his amazement, however, the priest looked at him pityingly and shook his head.

"You have had a nasty accident," he said, "and it has affected your head. You must not speak."

Not another word would he say in response to all the boy's eager queries. He simply ignored Elkanan who puzzled his head over the matter until he really began to feel ill and to wonder whether he was Elkanan after all. Tired out, he fell asleep again, and next time he awoke he was lying on a bed in a bare room. A bell was tolling, and he heard a chanting chorus. By his side stood a priest.

Elkanan looked at the priest like one dazed. Before he could utter a word, the priest said: "Rise, Andreas, and follow me."

The boy had no alternative but to obey. To his horror he was taken into a chapel and made to kneel. The priests sprinkled water on him. He did not understand what the service meant, and when it was over he began to cry for his father and mother. For days nobody took the slightest notice of his continual questionings until a priest, with a harsh, cruel face, spoke to him severely one day.

"I perceive, Andreas," he said, "thou hast a stubborn spirit. It shall be curbed. Thy father and mother are dead--all the world is dead to thee Thou hast strange notions in thy head. We shall rid thee of them."

Elkanan cried so much on hearing these terrible words that he made himself seriously ill.

How long he was kept in bed he knew not, but when he recovered, he found himself a prisoner in a monastery. All the priests called him Andreas, they were kind to him, and in time he began to doubt himself whether he was Elkanan, the son of Simon, the pious Jew of Mayence.

To put an end to the unrest in his mind, he devoted himself earnestly to his lessons. His tutors never had so brilliant a pupil, nor so intelligent a companion. He was a remarkable chess player.

"Where did you learn?" they asked him.

"My father, Simon ben Isaac, of Mayence, taught me," he replied, with a sob in his voice.

"It is well," they replied, having received their instructions what to say in answer to such remarks, "thou art blessed from Heaven, Andreas. Not only dost thou absorb learning in the hours of daylight, but angels and dead sages visit thee in they sleep and impart knowledge unto thee."

He could obtain no more satisfactory words from his tutors, and in time he made no mention whatever of the past, and his tutors and companions refrained from touching upon the subject either. Once or twice he formed the idea of endeavoring to escape, but he soon discovered the project impossible. He was never allowed to be alone for a moment; he was virtually a prisoner, although all men began to do him honor because of his amazing knowledge and learning.

In due time, he became a priest and a tutor and was even called to Rome and was created a cardinal. He wore a red cap and cloak, people kneeled to him and sought his blessing, and all spoke of him as the wisest, kindliest and most scholarly man in the Church.

He had not spoken of his boyhood for years, but he never ceased to think of those happy days. And although he tried hard, he could not believe that it was all a dream. Whenever he played a game of chess, which was his one pastime, he seemed to see himself in his old room at Mayence, and he sighed. His fellow priests wondered why he did this, and he laughingly told them it was because he had no idea how to lose a game.

Then a great event happened. The Pope died and Andreas was elected his successor. He was placed on a throne, a crown was put upon his head, and he was called Holy Father. The power of life and death over millions of people in many countries was vested in him; kings, princes and nobles visited him in his great palace to do him homage, and his fame spread far and wide. But he himself grew more thoughtful and silent and sought only to exercise his great powers for the people's good.

This, however, did not altogether please some of his counselors.

"The Church needs money," they told him. "We must squeeze it out of the Jews."

But Andreas steadfastly refused to countenance any persecutions. Many edicts were placed before him for his signature, giving permission to bishops in certain districts to threaten the Jews unless they paid huge sums of money in tribute, but Andreas declined to assent to any one of them.

One day a document was submitted to him from the archbishop of the Rhine district, craving permission to drive the Jews from the city of Mayence. The Pope's face hardened when he read the iniquitous letter. He gave instant orders that the archbishop should be summoned to Rome, and to the utter amazement of his cardinals he also commanded them to bring before him three leading Jews from Mayence, to state their case.

"It shall not be said," he declared, "that the Pope issued a decree of punishment without giving the people condemned an opportunity of defending themselves."

When the news reached Mayence there was great wailing and sorrow among the Jews, for, alas! bitter experience had taught them to expect no mercy from Rome. Delegates were selected, and when they arrived at the Vatican they were asked for their names. These were given and communicated to the Pope.

"The delegates of the Jews of the city of Mayence," announced a secretary, "humbly crave audience of Your Holiness."

"Their names?" demanded the Pope.

"Simon ben Isaac, Abraham ben Moses, and Issachar, the priest."

"Let them enter," said the Pope, in a quiet, firm voice. He had heard but one name; his plan had proved successful, for he had counted upon Simon being one of the chosen delegates.

The three men entered the audience chamber and stood expectant before the Pope. His Holiness appeared to be lost in deep thought. Suddenly he aroused himself from his reverie and looked keenly at the aged leader of the party.

"Simon of Mayence, stand forth," he said, "and give voice to thy plea. We give thee attention."

The old man approached a few paces nearer, and in simple, but eloquent language, pleaded that the Jews should be permitted to remain unmolested in Mayence in which city their community had been long established.

"Thy prayer" said the Pope, when he had finished, "shall have full consideration, and my answer shall be made known to thee without delay. Now tell me, Simon of Mayence, something of thyself and thy co-delegates. Who are ye in the city?"

Simon gave the information.

"Have ye come hither alone?" asked the Pope. "Or have ye been escorted by members of your families--your sons?"

The Pope's voice was scarcely steady, but none noticed.

"I have no son," said Simon, with a weary sigh.

"Hast thou never been blessed with offspring?"

Simon looked sharply at the Pope before answering. Then, with bowed head and broken voice, he said: "God blessed me with one son, but he was stolen from me in childhood. That has been the sorrow of my life.'

The old man's voice was choked with sobs.

"I have heard," said the Pope, after a while, "that thou art famed as a chess-player. I, too, am credited with some skill in the game. I would fain pit it against thine. Hearken! If thou prove the victor in the game, then shall thy appeal prevail."

"I consent," said the old man, proudly. "It is many years since I have sustained defeat."

It was arranged that the game should be played that evening. Naturally, the strange contest aroused the keenest interest. The game was followed closely by the papal secretaries and the Jewish delegates. It was a wonderful trial of subtle play. The two players seemed about evenly matched. First one and then the other made a daring move which appeared to place his opponent in difficulties, but each time disaster was ingeniously evaded. A draw seemed the likeliest result until, suddenly, the Pope made a brilliant move which startled the onlookers. It was considered impossible now for Simon to avoid defeat.

No one was more astounded at the Pope's move than the old Jew. He rose tremblingly from his chair, gazed with piercing eyes into the face of the Pope and said huskily, "Where didst thou learn that move? I taught it to but one other."

"Who?" demanded the Pope, eagerly. "I will tell thee alone," said Simon.

The Pope made a sign, and the others left the room in great surprise.

Then Simon exclaimed excitedly, "Unless thou art the devil himself, thou canst only be my long lost son, Elkanan."

"Father!" cried the Pope, and the old man clasped him in his arms.

When the others re-entered the room, the Pope said quietly, "We have decided to call the game a draw, and in thankfulness for the rare pleasure of a game of chess with so skilled a player as Simon of Mayence, I grant the prayer of the delegates of that city. It is my will that the Jews shall live in peace."

Shortly afterward, a new Pope was elected. Various rumors gained currency. One was that Andreas had thrown himself into the flames; another that he had mysteriously disappeared. And at the same time a stranger arrived in Mayence and was welcomed by Simon joyfully as his son, Elkanan.

THE SLAVE'S FORTUNE

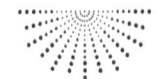

Ahmed was the only child of the wealthiest merchant in Damascus. His father devoted his days to doing everything possible to anticipate his wishes. The boy returned his father's love with interest, and the two lived together in the utmost happiness. They were seldom apart, the father curtailing his business journeys so that he could hastily return to Damascus, and finally restricting his affairs to those which he could perform in his own home.

For safety's sake, Ahmed, whenever he was out of his father's sight, was attended by a big negro slave, Pedro, an imposing looking person, richly attired as befitted his station and duties. Pedro was a faithful servant, and he and Ahmed were the firmest friends.

When Ahmed grew up to be a youth, his father decided to send him to Jerusalem to be educated. He did so reluctantly, knowing, however, that it was the wisest course to adopt,

Gently he broke the news to Ahmed, for he knew the latter would dislike to leave home. Ahmed was truly sorry to have to be parted from his father, but he kept back his tears and said bravely:

"It is thy wish, father, therefore I question it not. I know that thou desirest only my welfare."

"Well spoken, my son," said his father.

"May I take Pedro with me?" asked Ahmed.

"Nay, that would not be seemly," answered his father, gently. "It would make thee appear anxious to display thy wealth. Such ostentation will induce people to regard thee and thy father as foolish persons, possessed of more wealth than is good for the exercise of wisdom. Also, my son, thy future teaching must be not confined to the learning that wise men can impart unto thee. Thou art going to the great city to learn the ways of the world, to train thyself in self-reliance, and to prepare thyself for all the duties of manhood."

The youth was somewhat disappointed to hear this. It was the first occasion, as far as his memory served him, that his father had failed to grant his wish; but he was nevertheless flattered by the prospect of quickly becoming a man, and he answered, "I bow to thy wisdom, my father."

He left for Jerusalem, after bidding the merchant an affectionate farewell, and in the Holy City he applied himself diligently to his studies. He delighted his teachers with his cheerful attention to his lessons, and discovered a new source of happiness in learning things for himself from observation. Also, it was a pleasant sensation to conduct his own affairs, and in the great city, with its busy narrow thoroughfares and its wonderful buildings, he daily grew less homesick. Regularly he received letters by messengers from his father, and dutifully he returned, by the same means, long epistles, setting out all the big and little things that made up his life.

A year passed, and one day the usual message that Ahmed expected came to him in a strange hand-writing.

He opened it hastily, with a foreboding of evil and alarm. The writer of the letter was one of the merchant's closest friends. He said:

"O worthy son of a most worthy father, greeting to thee, and may God give thee strength to hear the terrible and sad tidings which it is my sorrowful duty to convey unto thee. Know then that it hath pleased God in his wisdom to call from this earth thy saintly father, to sit with the righteous ones in Heaven. Here in the city of Damascus there is great weeping, for thy honored father was the most upright of men, a friend to all in distress, a man whose bounteous charity to the poor and unfortunate was unsurpassed. But our grief, deep and heartfelt as it is, cannot be compared to thine. We have all lost a wise counselor, a trusty friend, a guide in all things. But thou hast lost more. Thou hast lost a father. Thou art his only son, and on thee his duties will now devolve. Know then thy profound grief we share with thee. We tender to thee our sincere sympathy, and eagerly do we await thy coming. Thou hast a noble position to occupy and a tradition to continue. We, thy father's friends and thine, O Ahmed, will assist thee."

The young man was dumbfounded when he gathered the purport of the letter. For some moments he spoke not, but sat on the ground, weeping silently. Then, remembering his father's admonitions, he promptly took up the task of settling his affairs in Jerusalem prior to his departure for Damascus.

"I will take with me," he said, "the good rabbi who has been my religious instructor, for I am not fully prepared to undertake all the duties that will fall to my lot and need some strengthening counsel."

On arrival at Damascus he was greeted by a large concourse of people who expressed their sympathy with him and spoke in terms of highest praise of his father's benevolence.

After the funeral, Ahmed called the leading townspeople together to hear his father's will read, for he was certain that many gifts to charities would be announced. Such was the case, and there were subdued murmurs of applause when the amounts were read forth.

Then suddenly the friend who had written to the young man and was reading the will, paused.

"I fear there must be a mistake," he said, in a whisper to Ahmed.

"Go on," urged the assembled people, and the man read in a strange voice:

"And now, having as I hope, faithfully performed my duty to the poor, I bequeath the rest of my possessions unto my devoted negro slave, Pedro."

"Pedro!" cried the astonished crowd.

They looked at the massive figure of the black attendant, but he stood motionless and impassive, betraying no sign whatsoever of joy or surprise.

Ahmed could not conceal his bewilderment. "Is naught left unto me?" he managed to ask.

"Yes," returned his friend, and amid a sudden silence, he continued to read: "This bequest is subject to the following proviso: that one thing be given to my son before the division of my property, the same to be selected by him within twenty-four hours of the reading of this will unto him."

The crowd melted away with mutterings of sympathy mingled with astonishment, but out of earshot of Ahmed, all said the merchant must have been mad to draw up so absurd a testament. Ahmed himself could hardly realize the great blow that had befallen him. He consulted with his father's friend and the rabbi, but, although they re-read the document many times, they could find no fault or flaw in it.

"Legally, this is correct and in perfect order and cannot be altered," said the friend.

"My father must have made a foolish mistake and must have misplaced the two words 'son' and 'slave,' " said Ahmed, bitterly.

"That does not so appear," said the rabbi; "thy father was a scholar and wise man. Speak not hastily, and above all act not rashly without thought. I would counsel thee to sleep over this matter, and in the morning we shall solve this puzzle."

Ahmed, who was exhausted with grief and rage and surprise, soon fell into a deep sleep, and when he awoke the rabbi was reciting his morning prayers.

"It is a beautiful day," he said, when he had finished. "The sun shines on thy happiness, Ahmed."

Ahmed was too depressed to make any comment, nor was he completely satisfied when the rabbi assured him all would be well.

"I have pondered deeply and long over thy father's words," he said. "I sat up through the night until the dawn, and I have been impelled to the conclusion that thy father was truly a wise man."

Ahmed interrupted with a gesture of disapproval. The rabbi took no notice but proceeded quietly: "Thy father must have feared that in thy absence after his death and pending thy possible delay in returning hither, slaves and others might rob thee of thy inheritance. Pedro, I have discovered, knew of the terms of the will.

By informing him and making his strange will, thy father, O fortunate Ahmed, made sure of thy inheritance unto thee."

"I understand not," muttered Ahmed.

"It is perfectly clear," said the rabbi. "As soon as thou art ready, thou shalt make thy choice of one thing. Do as I bid thee, and thou shalt see thy father's wisdom."

Ahmed had no option but to agree. He could find no solution himself, and wretched though he felt, reason told him that his father loved him and that the rabbi was renowned for shrewdness.

The townspeople gathered early to hear Ahmed make his choice of one thing--and one only--from his father's possessions. Ahmed looked less troubled than they expected, the rabbi wore his most benign expression, and Pedro stationed himself in his usual place at the door, statuesque, obedient, and expressionless as ever.

Ahmed held up his hand to obtain silence.

"Acting under the terms of my father's will," he said, solemnly, "at this moment when all, before division, belongs to his estate, I choose but one of my father's possessions--Pedro, the black slave."

Then everybody saw the wisdom of the strange will, for with Pedro, Ahmed became possessed of his father's vast wealth.

To Pedro, who still stood motionless, Ahmed said, "And thou, my good friend, shalt have thy freedom and possessions sufficient to keep thee in comfort for the rest of thy days."

"I desire naught but to serve thee," Pedro answered, "I wish to remain the faithful attendant of one who will follow nobly in the footsteps of thy father."

So everybody was satisfied.

THE PARADISE IN THE SEA

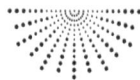

*H*iram, king of Tyre, was a foolish old man. He lived so long and grew to such a venerable age that he absurdly imagined he would never die. The idea gained strength daily in his mind and thus he mused:

"David, king of the Jews, I knew, and afterward his son, the wise King Solomon. But wise as he was, Solomon had to appeal to me for assistance in building his wondrous Temple, and it was only with the aid of the skilled workmen I sent to him that he successfully accomplished the erection of that structure. David, the sweet singer in Israel, who, as a mere boy slew the giant Goliath, has passed away. I still live. It must be that I shall never die. Men die. Gods live for ever. I must be a god, and why not?"

He put that question to the chief of his counselors, who, however, was much too wise to answer it. Now the counselors of the king had never yet failed to answer his queries, and so Hiram felt sure he had at last puzzled them by a question beyond the power of mortal man to answer. That was another proof, he told himself, that he was different from other men and kings--that, in short, he was a god.

"I must be, I must be," he muttered to himself, and he repeated this to himself so regularly that he came to the conclusion it was true.

"It is not I, but the voice of the Spirit of God that is in me that speaks," he said to himself, and he thought this remark so clever that he regarded it as still further proof. It is so easy to delude one's self.

Then he decided to make the great secret known to the people, and the doddering old man thought if he would do this in an unusual way, his subjects would have no doubts. He did not make a proclamation commanding everybody to believe in him as a god; he whispered the secret first to his chief counselor and instructed him to tell it to one person daily and to order all who were informed to do likewise. In this way the news soon spread to the remotest corners of the country, for if you work out a little sum you will discover that if you take the figure one and double it thus: two, four, eight, sixteen, and so on, it will run into millions.

In spite of this, nothing happened. Hiram, now quite idiotic, commanded the people to worship him. Some obeyed, fearing that if they refused they would be punished, or even put to death. Others declared there was no evidence that the king was a god. This came to the knowledge of Hiram and troubled him sorely.

"What proof do the unbelievers require?" he asked of his counselors.

They hesitated to reply, but presently the vizier, a shrewd old man with a long beard, said quietly, "I have heard people say a god must have a heaven from which to hurl lightning and thunderbolts, and a paradise in which to dwell."

"I shall have a heaven and a paradise," said Hiram, after a few moments' silence, adding to himself: "If Solomon could build a marvelous temple by the help of my workmen, surely I can devise a paradise."

He spent so much thought over this that it seemed to become easier each day. Besides, it would be so nice to live in a paradise all to himself. At first he decided to build a great big palace of gold, with windows of precious stones. There would be a high tower on which the throne would be placed so far above the people that they must be impressed with the fact that he was God.

Then it occurred to him this would not do. A palace, however vast and beautiful, would only be a building, not a paradise. Day and night he pondered and worried until his head ached badly. Then one day, while watching a ship on the sea, an extraordinary idea came into his head.

"I will build a palace which will seem to hang above the water on nothing!" he said to himself, chuckling. "None but a god could conceive such a brilliant idea."

Hiram set about his ingenious plan at once. He sent trusted envoys far and wide for skilled divers. Only those who did not know the language of the country were selected. Hiram himself gave them their orders and they worked only at night, so that none should see or know of their work. Their task was to fasten four huge pillars to the bottom of the sea. Their work completed, the divers were well paid and sent away.

Next, a different gang of workmen was brought from a strange land. They constructed a platform on the pillars in the sea. Then a third lot of artisans began to erect a wonderful edifice on the platform. They, too, only worked at night, but the building could no longer be concealed. It was showing itself above the sea. The people were therefore told, by royal proclamation, in these words:

> I, Hiram of Tyre, the King, and of all the People,
> GOD OMNIPOTENT,
> Hereby make known to you that it has become my pleasure to reveal unto you my
> PARADISE
> which hitherto I have concealed in the clouds. Ye who are worthy shall behold it
> TODAY!

Of all the clever things he had done, Hiram believed the composition of that proclamation the cleverest.

"Those who do not see, will think themselves unworthy," he said, "and will tremble in fear of my wrath. They will see a little more each day and will think themselves growing worthy. And they will believe; they must, when they see it all. Besides, they will look upward, toward the clouds, to see the paradise descending. They will never think of looking below to see it rising."

And so it happened. The people could not help but be impressed when they saw the amazing structure. It grew daily, apparently of its own accord, for no workmen were seen; and most wonderful of all, it seemed to rest on nothing in the air!

This was because the first story was of clearest glass, so clear, indeed, that the people saw through it and thought they saw nothing. On this the other stories were erected, and, of course, they appeared to be suspended in space.

There were seven stories to represent seven heavens. The second, the one above the glass, was constructed of iron, the third was of lead, the fourth of shining brass, the fifth of burnished copper, the sixth of glistening silver, and the last story of all, of pure gold.

The whole building was lavishly studded with precious stones, gems and jewels of many hues. By day, when the sun shone and was reflected from the thousands of jewels and the polished metals, the appearance was dazzling; the people could not help but regard as a heaven that which they could scarcely look upon without being blinded. In the setting sun the uppermost story, with its huge golden dome, glowed like an expanse of fire; and by night, the myriad gems twinkled like additional stars.

Yet some people would not believe this was a paradise, and so Hiram had to set his wits to work again.

"Thunder and lightning I must produce," he said, and this part of his ambition he found not at all difficult.

In the second story he kept huge boulders and round heavy stones. When these were rolled about the people thought the noise was thunder. By means of many revolving windows and reflectors, Hiram could flash a light on the town and delude simple people, who were easily impressed and frightened, into the belief that they saw lightning.

"When I am seated here above the forces of the storm," said Hiram, "the people must surely accept me as God and extol me above all mortal kings."

He was foolishly happy on his throne in the clouds, but his counselors shook their heads. They knew that such folly would meet with its due punishment. They warned Hiram against remaining in his paradise during a storm, but he replied, in a rage: "I, the God of the storm, am not afraid."

But when the real thunder rolled and the lightning flashed all around his paradise, Hiram lost his boastful courage. He saw visions. Trembling in every limb, he crouched on his throne and imagined he saw angels and demons and fairies dancing round him and jeering at his pretensions and his wonderful structure.

The storm grew fiercer, the lightning more vivid, the thunder-crashes louder, and Hiram screamed when there was a tremendous noise of crashing glass. The first story could not withstand the terrible buffeting of the waves. It cracked and crumbled. There was no support left for the six heavens above. They could no longer hang in space.

With a mighty crash, that struck terror into the hearts of the beholders, the whole structure collapsed in a thousand pieces in the sea.

Marvelous to relate, Hiram was not killed or drowned. It seemed a miracle that he should be saved, but such was the case; and some people thought that proved him to be a god more than his unfortunate paradise. But his life was only spared to end in greater misery and sorrow. He was dethroned by Nebuchadnezzar and ended his days a wretched captive. And all the people knew that Hiram, once the great king of Tyre, the friend of King David and King Solomon, was but a mortal and a foolish one.

THE RABBI'S BOGEY-MAN

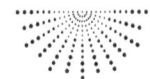

Rabbi Lion, of the ancient city of Prague, sat in his study in the Ghetto looking very troubled. Through the window he could see the River Moldau with the narrow streets of the Jewish quarter clustered around the cemetery, which still stands to-day, and where is to be seen this famous plan's tomb. Beyond the Ghetto rose the towers and spires of the city, but just at that moment it was not the cruelty of the people to the Jews that occupied the rabbi's thoughts. He was unable to find a servant, even one to attend the fire on the Sabbath for him.

The truth was that the people were a little afraid of the rabbi. He was a very learned man, wise and studious, and a scientist; and because he did wonderful things people called him a magician. His experiments in chemistry frightened them. Late at nights they saw little spurts of blue and red flame shine from his window, and they said that demons and witches came at his beck and call. So nobody would enter his service.

"If, as they declare, I am truly a magician," he said to himself, "why should I not make for myself a servant, one that will tend the fire for me on the Sabbath?"

He set to work on his novel idea and in a few weeks had completed his mechanical creature, a woman. She looked like a big, strong, laboring woman, and the rabbi was greatly pleased with his handiwork.

"Now to endow it with life," he said.

Carefully, in the silence of his mysterious study at midnight, he wrote out the Unpronounceable Sacred Name of God on a piece of parchment. Then he rolled it up and placed it in the mouth of the creature.

Immediately it sprang up and began to move like a living thing. It rolled its eyes, waved its arms, and nearly walked through the window. In alarm, Rabbi Lion snatched the parchment from its mouth and the creature fell helpless to the floor.

"I must be careful," said the rabbi. "It is a wonderful machine with its many springs and screws and levers, and will be most useful to me as soon as I learn to control it properly."

All the people marveled when they saw the rabbi's machine-woman running errands and doing many duties, controlled only by his thoughts. She could do everything but speak, and Rabbi Lion discovered that he must take the Name from her mouth before he went to sleep. Otherwise, she might have done mischief.

One cold Sabbath afternoon, the rabbi was preaching in the synagogue and the little children stood outside his house looking at the machine-woman seated by the window. When they rolled their eyes she did, and at last they shouted: "Come and play with us."

She promptly jumped through the window and stood among the boys and girls.

"We are cold," said one. "Canst thou make a fire for us?"

The creature was made to obey orders, so she at once collected sticks and lit a fire in the street. Then, with the children, she danced round the blaze in great glee. She piled on all the sticks and old barrels she could find, and soon the fire spread and caught a house. The children ran away in fear while the fire blazed so furiously that the whole town became alarmed. Before the flames could be extinguished, a number of houses had been burned down and much damage done. The creature could not be found, and only when the parchment with the Name, which could not burn, was discovered amid the ashes, was it known that she had been destroyed in the conflagration.

The Council of the city was indignant when it learned of the strange occurrence, and Rabbi Lion was summoned to appear before King Rudolf.

"What is this I hear," asked his majesty. "Is it not a sin to make a living creature?"

"It had no life but that which the Sacred Name gave it," replied the rabbi.

"I understand it not," said the king. "Thou wilt be imprisoned and must make another creature, so that I may see it for myself. If it is as thou sayest, thy life shall be spared. If not--if, in truth, thou profanest God's sacred law and makest a living thing, thou shalt die and all thy people shall be expelled from this city."

Rabbi Lion at once set to work, and this time made a man, much bigger than the woman that had been burned.

"As your majesty sees," said the rabbi, when his task was completed, "it is but a creature of wood and glue with springs at the joints. Now observe," and he put the Sacred Name in its mouth.

Slowly the creature rose to its feet and saluted the monarch who was so delighted that he cried: "Give him to me, rabbi."

"That cannot be," said Rabbi Lion, solemnly. "The Sacred Name must not pass from my possession. Otherwise the creature may do great damage again. This time I shall take care and will not use the man on the Sabbath."

The king saw the wisdom of this and set the rabbi at liberty and allowed him to take the creature to his house. The Jews looked on in wonderment when they saw the creature walking along the street by the side of Rabbi Lion, but the children ran away in fear, crying: "The bogey-man."

The rabbi exercised caution with his bogey-man this time, and every Friday, just before Sabbath commenced, he took the name from its mouth so as to render it powerless.

It became more wonderful every day, and one evening it startled the rabbi from a doze by beginning to speak.

"I want to be a soldier," it said, "and fight for the king. I belong to the king. You made me for him."

"Silence," cried Rabbi Lion, and it had to obey. "I like not this," said the rabbi to himself.

"This monster must not become my master, or it may destroy me and perhaps all the Jews."

He could not help but wonder whether the king was right and that it must be a sin to create a man. The creature not only spoke, but grew surly and disobedient, and yet the rabbi hesitated to break it up, for it was most useful to him. It did all his cooking, washing and cleaning, and three servants could not have performed the work so neatly and quickly.

One Friday afternoon when the rabbi was preparing to go to the synagogue, he heard a loud noise in the street.

"Come quickly," the people shouted at his door. "Your bogey-man is trying to get into the synagogue."

Rabbi Lion rushed out in a state of alarm. The monster had slipped from the house and was battering down the door of the synagogue.

"What art thou doing?" demanded the rabbi, sternly.

"Trying to get into the synagogue to destroy the scrolls of the Holy Law," answered the monster. "Then wilt thou have no power over me, and I shall make a great army of bogey-men who shall fight for the king and kill all the Jews."

"I will kill thee first," exclaimed Rabbi Lion, and springing forward he snatched the parchment with the Name so quickly from the creature's mouth that it collapsed at his feet a mass of broken springs and pieces of wood and glue.

For many years afterward these pieces were shown to visitors in the attic of the synagogue when the story was told of the rabbi's bogey-man.

THE FAIRY FROG

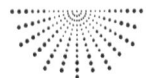

Once upon a time there lived a man of learning and wealth who had an only son, named Hanina. To this son, who was grown up and married, he sent a messenger asking that he should immediately come to his father. Hanina obeyed, and found both his father and mother lying ill.

"Know, my son," said the old man, "we are about to die. Grieve not, for it has been so ordained. We have been companions through life, and we are to be privileged to leave this world together. You will mourn for us the customary seven days. They will end on the eve of the festival of the Passover. On that day go forth into the market place and purchase the first thing offered to thee, no matter what it is, or what the cost that may be demanded. It will in due course bring thee good fortune. Hearken unto my words, my son, and all will be well."

Hanina promised obedience to this strange injunction of his father, and events fell out in accordance with the old man's prediction. The aged couple died on the same day, were buried together and after the week of mourning, on the day preceding the Passover festival, Hanina made his way to the market place wondering what adventure was in store for him.

He had scarcely entered the market place, where all manner of wares were displayed, when an old man approached him, carrying a silver casket of curious design.

"Purchase this, my son," he said, "and it will bring thee good fortune."

"What does it contain?" asked Hanina.

"That I may not inform thee," was the reply. "Indeed I cannot, for I know not. Only the purchaser can open it at the feast which begins the Passover."

Naturally, Hanina was impressed by these words. Matters were shaping just as his father foretold.

"What is the price?" he asked.

"A thousand gold pieces."

That was an enormous sum, nearly the whole that he possessed, but Hanina, remembering his vow, paid the money and took the casket home.

It was placed upon the table that night when the Passover festival began. On being opened it was found to contain a smaller casket. This was opened and out sprang a frog.

Hanina's wife was sorely disappointed, but she gave food to the frog which devoured everything greedily. So much did the creature eat that when the Passover had ended, in eight days it had grown to an enormous size. Hanina built a cabinet for his strange possession, but it continued to grow and soon required a special shed.

Hanina was seriously puzzled, for the frog ate so ravenously that he and his wife had little food for themselves. But they made no complaint, although their hardships increased daily. They were compelled to dispose of almost everything they possessed to keep the frog supplied with food, and at last they were left in a state of abject poverty. Then only did the courage of Hanina's wife give way and she began to cry.

To her astonishment, the frog, which was now bigger than a man, spoke to her.

"Listen to me, wife of the faithful Hanina," it said. "Ye have treated me well. Therefore, ask of me what ye will, and I shall carry out your wishes."

"Give us food," sobbed the woman.

"It is there," said the frog, and at that very moment there was a knock at the door and a huge basket of food was delivered.

Hanina had not yet spoken, and the frog asked him to name his desire.

"A frog that speaks and performs wonders must be wise and learned," said Hanina. "I wish that thou shouldst teach me the lore of men."

The frog agreed, and his method of teaching was exceedingly strange. He wrote out the Law and the seventy known languages on strips of paper. These he ordered Hanina to swallow. Hanina did so and became acquainted with everything, even the language of the beasts and the birds. All men regarded him as the most learned sage of his time.

One day the frog spoke again.

"The day has arrived," he said, "when I must repay you for all the kindness you have shown me. Your reward shall be great. Come with me to the woods and you shall see marvels performed."

Hanina and his wife followed the giant frog to the woods very early one morning, and a comical figure it presented as it hobbled along.

Arrived at the woods, the frog cried out, in its croaking voice:

"Come to me all ye inhabitants of the trees, the caves and streams, and do my bidding. Bring precious stones from the depths of the earth and roots and herbs."

Then began the queerest procession. Hundreds upon hundreds of birds came twittering through the trees; thousands upon thousands of insects came crawling from holes in the ground; and all the animals in the woods, from the tiniest to the monsters, came in answer to the call of the frog. Each group brought some gift and laid it at the feet of Hanina and his wife who stood in some alarm. Soon a great pile of precious stones and herbs was heaped before them.

"All these belong to you," said the frog, pointing to the jewels. "Of equal worth are the herbs and the roots with which ye can cure all diseases. Because ye obeyed the wishes of the dying and did not question me, ye are now rewarded."

Hanina and his wife thanked the frog and then the former said: "May we not know who thou art?"

"Yes," replied the frog. "I am the fairy son of Adam, gifted with the power of assuming any form. Farewell."

With these words, the frog began to grow smaller and smaller until it was the size of an ordinary frog. Then it hopped into a stream and disappeared and all the denizens of the woods returned to their haunts.

Hanina and his wife made their way home with their treasures. They became famous for their wealth, their wisdom and their charity, and lived in happiness with all peoples for many, many years.

THE PRINCESS OF THE TOWER

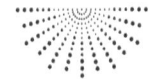

I

*P*rincess Solima was sick, not exactly ill, but so much out of sorts that her father, King Zuliman, was both annoyed and perturbed. The princess was as beautiful as a princess of those days should be; her long tresses were like threads of gold, her blue eyes rivaled the color of the sky on the balmiest summer day; and her smile was as radiant as the sunshine itself.

She was learned and clever, too, and her goodness of heart gained for her as great a renown as her peerless beauty. Despite all this, Princess Solima was not happy. Indeed, she was wretched to despondency, and her melancholy weighed heavily upon her father.

"What ails you, my precious daughter?" he asked her a hundred times, but she made no answer.

She just sat and silently moped. She did not waste away, which puzzled the physicians; she did not grow pale, which surprised her attendants; and she did not weep, which astonished herself. But she felt as if her heart had grown heavy, as if there was no use in anything.

The king squared his shoulders to show his determination and summoned his magicians and wizards and sorcerers and commanded them to perform their arts and solve the mystery of the illness of Princess Solima. A strange crew they were, ranged in a semi-circle before the king. There was the renowned astrologer from Egypt, a little man with a humpback; the mixer of mysterious potions from China, a long, lank yellow man, with tiny eyes; the alchemist from Arabia, a scowling man with his face almost concealed by whiskers; there was a Greek and a Persian and a Phoenician, each with some special knowledge and fearfully anxious to display it. They set to work.

One studied the stars, another concocted a sweet-smelling fluid, a third retired to the woods and thought deeply, a fourth made abstruse calculations with diagrams and figures, a fifth questioned the princess' handmaidens, and a sixth conceived the brilliant notion of talking with the princess herself. He was certainly an original wizard, and he learned more than all the others.

Then they met in consultation and talked foreign languages and pretended very seriously to understand one another. One said the stars were in opposition, another said he had gazed into a crystal and had seen a glow-worm chasing a hippopotamus which a third interpreted as meaning the princess would die if the glow-worm won the race.

"Rubbish!" exclaimed the magician who had spoken to the princess; "likewise stuff and nonsense and the equivalent thereof in the seventy unknown languages."

That was an impertinent comment on their divinations, and so they listened seriously.

"The princess," he said, "is just tired. That is a disease which will become popular and fashionable as the world grows older and more people amass riches. She is sick of being waited on hand and foot and bowed down to and all that sort of thing. She has never been allowed to romp as a child, to choose her own companions and the rest of it. Therefore, she is bored with all the etceteras. The case is comprehensible and comprehensive: it needs the exercise of imagination stimulated by prescience, conscience, patience...."

The others yawned and began to collect dictionaries, and fearing that they might be tempted to fling them at him after they had found the meaning of his big words, he ceased.

"I agree," said the president of the assembly, the oldest wizard, "only I diagnose the disease in simpler form. The princess is in love."

That set them all jabbering together, and they finally agreed to report to the king that the time had arrived when the princess should marry, so that she should be able to go away to a new land, amid other people and different scenes.

The king agreed reluctantly, for he dearly loved his daughter and wished her to remain with him always if possible. Heralds and messengers were sent out far and wide, and very soon a procession of suitors for the princess' hand began to file past the lady. They were princes of all shapes and sizes, of all complexions and colors; some were resplendent with jewels, others were followed by retinues of slaves bearing gifts; a few entered the competition by proxy--that is, they sent somebody else to see the lady first and pronounce judgment upon her. These she dismissed summarily, declaring that they were disqualified by the rules of fair play.

When all the entrants had been inspected by the king, he said to his daughter:

"Pick the one you love the best, Solima dear."

"None," she answered promptly.

"Dear, dear me--that is very awkward. We shall have to return the entrance fees--I mean the presents," he said.

That prospect did not seem to worry the princess in the least; nor did her father's appeal not to belittle him in the eyes of his fellow monarchs have the slightest effect on her.

"At least," he said, growing impatient, "tell me what you do want."

"I will marry any man," she replied, while he wondered gravely what else she could have said, "who is not such a fool as to think himself the only person in the world who is of consequence."

The king was not without wisdom, and he knew that this remark is foolish, or sensible, according to the mood in which it is said, and the thoughts behind it.

"You do not regard any one of the princes," the king said gently, "as worthy of ------"

"Any woman," interrupted his daughter. "Listen, my father, you have tried to make me happy always and until recently you have succeeded. I wish to obey you in all things, even in the choice of a husband. Would you really have me marry any one of these fools? Be not angry. Did any one reveal a gleam of wisdom, or common-sense? Were they not all just ridiculous fops? Let me enumerate:

"There was Prince Hafiz who talked only of his wars--of the men--aye and women and children--his soldiers had butchered. The soldiers fought and Prince Hafiz posed before me as a warrior and hero. I will not be queen in a land where people cannot live in peace.

"Then there was Prince Aziz who boasted that he spends all his life with his horses and dogs and falcons in the hunting field. He knows the needs of beasts, but not of men. I will not be the bride of a prince who allows his subjects to starve in wretchedness and poverty while he enjoys himself with the slaughter of wild beasts.

"Prince Guzman had nothing else to impart to me but his taste in jewels and dress. Prince Abdul knew exactly how many bottles of wine he drank daily, but he could not tell me how many schools there were in his city. Prince Hassan had not the slightest notion how the majority of his people lived, whether by trading, or thieving, or working, or begging."

King Zuliman listened intently. This was a singular speech for a princess, but reason told him this was profoundest wisdom.

"Oh, I am tired," burst out Princess Solima, in tears. "I have no desire for life if to be a ruler over men and women and children means that you must take no interest in their welfare. My father, hearken. I will not be queen in a land where the king thinks the people live only to make him great. I shall be proud and happy to reign where the king understands that it is his duty to make his people happy and his country prosperous and peaceful."

The king left his daughter, and, deeply concerned, sought his wizards.

"My daughter has been born thousands of years before her time," he declared, petulantly. "The stars have played a trick on me, and have sent me my great-great-great-great ever so much great granddaughter out of her turn."

The magicians did not laugh at this: they thought it a wonderfully sage remark, and after much mysterious whispering among themselves and consultation of old books, and gazing into crystals, they informed the king that the stars foretold that Princess Solima would marry a poor man!

They flattered themselves on their cleverness in arriving at this conclusion, which they deduced from the princess' contempt for princes.

King Zuliman's patience was exhausted by this time. In a towering rage, he told his daughter what the wizards had said, and when she merely said, "How nice," he swore he would imprison her in his fortress in the sea.

His majesty meant it, too, and at once had the fortress, which stood on a tiny island miles from land, luxuriously furnished and fitted up for his daughter's reception. Thither she was conveyed secretly one night, but to her father's disgust she made no protest.

"I shall be free for a while," she said, "of all the absurd flummery of the palace."

II.

The people were sad when the princess disappeared. She had been good and kind to them, had understood them, and they did not know whether she had died, or had deserted them without a word of farewell, though that was hardly possible. All that they knew was that the king suddenly became morose and sullen. Strangely enough, he began to take an interest in the poor. He asked them funny questions--for a king. How did they earn money? What was their occupation? Had they any pleasures? And what were their thoughts?

Young people laughed, but old men said the king intended to promote laws which would do good. Anyway, the king's interest did make his subjects happier, and the officers of state became very busy with projects and schemes for improving trade, providing work and for educating children.

"They do say," remarked one old woman, who kept an apple stall in the market place, "that a law will be passed that the sun should shine every day, and that it should never rain on the days of the market. Ah! that will be good," and she rubbed her hands at the prospect of not having to crouch under a leaky awning when the rain came pelting down, or over a tiny fire in a brass bowl in the winter, to thaw her frozen and benumbed hands.

Even the laborers in the fields, who were mainly dull-witted people with no learning whatsoever, heard the news; and they actually pondered over it and wondered whether it meant that they would never more be hungry and wretchedly clad.

One who thought deeply was a shepherd lad. He loved to bask lazily in the sun, to listen to the birds chirruping, and to all the sounds of the air and the fields and the forests. He seemed to understand them; the murmuring of the brooks on a warm day was like a gentle cradle song lulling him to sleep; on a day when the wind howled, its sulky growl as it dashed over the stones warned him that floods might come, and that he must move his flocks to safer ground.

"I wonder," he mused, "if I shall learn to read the written word and even to pen it myself. I could then write the song of the brook and the birds, so that others should know it."

And musing thus, he fell asleep. He slept longer than usual, and when he awoke, he was alarmed to see that the sun had set. Darkness was falling fast, and he had his flock to see safely home. The cows and sheep had begun to collect themselves as a matter of habit, and it was their noise that woke him. They were already trudging the well-known route, and all he had to do in following was to see that none strayed, or tumbled into the brook.

All went well until he came in sight of home. Then a huge bird, a ziz, bigger than several houses, appeared in the sky and swooped down on the cows and sheep.

The shepherd beat the monster off as long as he could with a big stick, while the affrighted animals scampered hastily homeward. The ziz however, was evidently determined not to be balked of its prey. It dug its talons deep into the flanks of an ox that had stampeded in the wrong direction and was lagging behind the others.

The poor animal bellowed in pain, and the shepherd, rushing to the rescue, seized it by the forelegs as it was being raised from the ground. Curling his leg round the slender trunk of a tree, the young man began a struggle with the ziz. The mighty bird, its eyes glowing like two signal lamps, tried to strike at him with his tremendous beak, one stroke of which would have been fatal.

In the fast gathering darkness it missed, fortunately for the shepherd, but the thrust of the beak caught the upper part of the tree trunk. It snapped under the blow, and the shepherd was compelled to release his hold. He still gripped tightly the forelegs of the ox, but with naught now to hold it back, the great bird had no difficulty in rising into the air. Before he fully grasped what had happened, the shepherd found himself high above the trees.

To release his hold would have meant destruction. He held on grimly, clutching the legs of the ox with all his might, and even swinging tip his feet to grip the hind-legs of the animal.

Higher and higher the ziz rose into the air, spreading its vast wings majestically, and flying silently and swiftly over the land. It made the shepherd giddy to glance down at the ground scurrying rapidly past far below him. So he closed his eyes, but opening them again for a moment, he was horrified to notice that the bird was now flying over the sea on which the moon was shining with silvery radiance. With a heavy sigh he gave himself up for lost, and began to consider whether it would be better to release his hold and fall down and be drowned, rather than be devoured by the gigantic bird.

Before he could make up his mind, the bird stopped, and the shepherd was bumped down on something with such violence that for a moment he was stunned. Looking around, when he re-gained his senses, he saw that he was on the top of a tower in the sea. Beside him was the carcass of the ox. Above them stood the ziz, its eyes glowing like twin fires, its beak thrust down o strike.

With a quick movement, the shepherd drew a knife which he carried in his girdle, and struck at the opening of the descending beak. The bird uttered a shrill cry of pain as the knife pierced its tongue, and in a few moments it had disappeared in the air. So swift was its flight that almost instantly it was a mere speck in the moon-lit sky.

Thoroughly exhausted, the shepherd slept until awakened by the sound of a voice. Opening his eyes, he saw that the sun had risen. Above him stood a woman of ravishing beauty. He sprang to his feet and bowed low.

"Who are you?" asked Princess Solima, for she it was. "And tell me how came you here with this carcass of an ox, so distant from the land, so high up as this tower in the sea?"

"Of a truth I scarcely know," answered the shepherd. "It may be that I am bewitched, or dreaming, for my adventure passes all belief," and he related it.

The princess made no comment, but motioned to him that he should follow her. He did so and she placed food before him. He was ravenously hungry and did full justice to the meal. Then she led him to the bath chamber.

"Wash and robe thyself," she said, giving him some clothes, "and then I have much to inquire of thee."

The shepherd felt ever so much better when he had bathed, and then attired in the strange garments she had given him, he appeared before the princess.

She gazed at him so long and searchingly that he blushed in confusion.

"Thou art fair to look upon and of manly stature," said the princess.

The shepherd could only stammer a reply, but after a while he said, "Fair lady, who and what thou art I know not. Such beauty as thine is the right of princesses only. I am but a poor shepherd."

"And may not a shepherd be handsome?" she asked. "Tell me: who hath laid down a law that only royal personages may be fair to behold? I have seen princes of vile countenance."

She stopped suddenly, for she did not wish to betray her secret. They sat in a little room in the tower, unknown to the many guards down below, and, although the shepherd protested, the princess waited on him herself, bringing him food, and cushions on which he could rest that night.

Next morning they ascended the tower together.

"I come here every morning," said the princess.

"Why?" the shepherd asked.

"To see if my husband cometh," was the answer.

"Who is he?" asked the shepherd.

The princess laughed.

"I know not," she said. "Some mornings when I have stood here and grieved at my loneliness, I have felt inclined to make a vow that I would marry the first man who came hither."

The shepherd was silent. Then he looked boldly into the princess' eyes and said: "Thou hast told me I am the first man who has come to thee. I am emboldened to declare my love for thee, a feeling that swept over me the moment my eyes beheld thee. Who thou art, what thou art, I know not, I care not. Shall we be husband and wife?"

The princess gave him her hand.

"It is ordained," she said, and thus their troth was plighted.

"We cannot remain here forever," said the princess, presently. "Canst thou, husband of my heart's choice, devise some means of escape?"

He looked down at the carcass of the ox thoughtfully for a few moments.

"I have it," he exclaimed, excitedly. "It is a safe assumption that the monster bird that brought me will return for his meal. He can then carry us away. If the heavens approve," he said, fervently, "thus it shall he."

That very night the ziz returned and feasted on the ox, and while it was fully occupied appeasing its hunger, the shepherd managed to attach strong ropes to its legs. To this he attached a large basket in which he and his bride made themselves comfortable with cushions. Nor did they forget to take a store of food.

Toward morning the ziz rose slowly into the air, and the lovers clutched each other tightly as the basket spun round and round. The giant bird did not seem to notice its burden at all, and after a moment it began a swift flight over the sea. After many hours a city became visible, and as it was approached the shepherd could note the excitement caused by the appearance of the ziz. The bird was getting tired, and having at last noticed the weight tied to its feet was evidently seeking to get rid of it.

Flying low it dashed the basket against a tower. The occupants feared they might be killed, but suddenly the cords snapped, the basket rested on the parapet of the tower, and the bird flew swiftly away.

No sooner had the shepherd extricated himself and his bride from the basket, than armed guards appeared. At sight of the princess they lowered their weapons and fell upon their faces.

"Inform my father I have returned," she said, and they immediately rose to do her bidding.

"Know you where you are?" asked the shepherd.

"Yes; this is the king's palace," was the reply.

Soon the king appeared, and with almost hysterical joy he embraced his daughter.

"I am happy to see thee again," he cried. "I crave thy pardon for immuring thee in the sea fortress. Thou shalt tell me all thy adventures."

Then he caught sight of the shepherd.

"Who is this?" he demanded.

"Thy son-in-law, my husband," said the princess, her joy showing in her bright eyes.

"What prince art thou?" asked the king.

"A prince among men," answered the princess quickly. "A man without riches, who comes from the people and will teach us their needs and how to rule them."

The king bowed to the inevitable. He blessed his son-in-law and daughter, appointed them to rule over a province, and they settled down to make everybody thoroughly happy, contented and prosperous.

PART I
KING ALEXANDER'S ADVENTURES

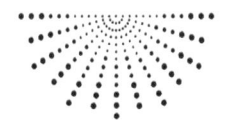

I. THE VISION OF VICTORY

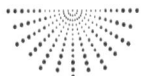

More than two thousand years ago there lived a king in the land of Macedon who was a great conqueror, and when his son, Alexander, was born, the soothsayers and the priestesses of the temples predicted that he would be a greater warrior than his father. Alexander was a wonderful boy, and his father, King Philip, was very proud of him when he tamed a spirited horse which nobody else could manage. The wisest philosophers of the day were Alexander's teachers, and when he was only sixteen years of age, Philip left him in charge of the country when he went to subdue Byzantium. Alexander was only twenty when he ascended the throne, but before then he had suppressed a rebellion and had proved himself possessed of exceptional daring and courage.

"I shall conquer the whole world," he said.

and although he only reigned thirteen years and died at the age of thirty-three, he accomplished his ambition. All the countries which were then known had to acknowledge his supremacy.

King Alexander was a drunkard and very cruel, but he treated the Jews kindly. When they heard he had been victorious over Darius, king of Persia, who was their ruler, and that he was marching on Jerusalem, they became seriously alarmed. Jadua, the high priest, however, counseled the people to welcome Alexander with great ceremony.

All the priests and the Levites donned their most gorgeous robes, the populace put on their holiday garb, and the streets of the city were gaily decorated with many colored banners and garlands of flowers. The night before Alexander arrived at the head of his army, a long procession was formed of the priests, the Levites, and the elders of the city, each carrying a lighted torch. At the gates of the city they awaited the approach of the mighty warrior.

In the early morning, before the sun had risen, Alexander made his appearance and was astonished at the magnificent spectacle which met his gaze. At the head of the procession' stood the high priest in his shining white robes, with the jewels of the ephod glittering on his breast. To the surprise of his generals, Alexander descended from his horse and bowed low before the high priest.

"Like unto an angel dost thou appear to me," he said.

"Let thy coming bring peace," replied Jadua.

Parmenio, the chief of Alexander's generals, had promised the soldiers rich store of plunder in Jerusalem, and he approached the king and said:

"Wherefore do you honor this priest of the Jews above all men?"

"I will tell thee," answered Alexander. "In dreams have I often seen this dignified priest. Ever he bade me be of good courage and always did he predict victory for me. Shall I not then pay homage to my guardian angel?"

Turning to the priest, he said, "Lead me to your Temple that I may offer up thanksgiving to the God of my guardian angel."

It was now daylight, and the priests walked in procession before King Alexander past cheering multitudes of people. At the Temple the king removed his sandals, but the priests gave him a pair of jeweled slippers, fearing that he might slip on the pavement. The king was pleased with all that he saw and desired that a statue of himself, or a portrait, should be placed in the holy building.

"That may not be," replied the high priest, "but in honor of thy visit all the boys born in Jerusalem this year shall be named Alexander."

"It is well," said the king, much pleased; "ask of me what you will, and if it be in my power I shall grant it."

"Mighty monarch," said Jadua, "we desire naught but to be permitted to serve our God according to our laws. Permit us to practice our religious observances free and unhindered. Grant also this privilege to the Jews who dwell in all thy dominions, and we shall ever pray for thy long life and triumph."

"It is but little that ye ask," replied the king, "and that little is easily granted."

The people cheered loudly when they heard the good news, and many Jews enrolled themselves in the army.

I. THE VISION OF VICTORY | 143

Alexander stayed some time in Jerusalem, and messengers arrived from Canaan to ask him to compel the Jews to restore them their land.

"It is written in the Books of Moses," they said, "that Canaan and its boundaries belong to the Canaanites."

Gebiah, a hunchback, undertook to answer.

"It is also written in the Books of Moses," he said, "'Cursed be Canaan; a servant shall he be unto his brethren.' The property of a slave belongs to his master, therefore Canaan is ours."

Alexander gave the envoys of Canaan three days in which to reply to this, but they fled from Jerusalem.

Messengers from Egypt came next, asking for the return of the gold and silver taken by the Israelites from the land of Pharaoh.

"What says Gebiah to this?" asked Alexander.

"We shall return the gold and silver," answered the hunchback, "when we have been paid for the many, many years of labor of our ancestors in Egypt."

"Truly a wise answer," said Alexander, and he gave the Egyptians three days to consider it. But they also fled.

When Alexander left Jerusalem he sought the advice of the wise men of Israel.

"I desire," he said, "to conquer the land beyond the Mountains of Darkness in Africa; it is also my wish to fly above the clouds and behold the heavens, and also to descend into the depths of the sea and gaze with mine own eyes on the monsters of the deep."

How to accomplish these things he was instructed by the wise men, but they warned him never to enter Babylon.

"For shouldst thou ever enter the city of Babylon," they said, "thou wilt assuredly die."

King Alexander thanked them for the advice and the warning, and set forth on his adventures.

II. THE LAND OF DARKNESS AND THE GATE OF PARADISE

*A*fter many days King Alexander came to the Mountains of Darkness. Acting on the advice of the wise men, he had provided himself with asses from the land of Libya, for they have the power of seeing in the dark, and also with a cord of great length. Mounted on the asses, he and his men plunged into the realms of darkness, unwinding the cord as they went, so that they might find their way back with it.

Around them was blackest darkness and a silence that inspired the men with awe. The asses, however, picked their way through the tall trees that grew so high and so thick that not the least ray of light could penetrate. How many days they traveled thus they knew not, for day and night were alike. The men slept when they were tired, ate when they were hungry and trusted to the asses and the cord.

At last when they emerged into the light they were almost blinded by the sun, and it was some time before they could see properly. Then, to their great astonishment, they found that there were no men in the land, only women, tall and finely proportioned, clothed in skins and armed with bows and arrows.

"Who are ye?" asked Alexander.

"We are the Amazons, women who are skilled in war and in the art of hunting," they answered.

"Lead me to your queen," commanded Alexander, "and bid her surrender, for I am Alexander, the Great, of Macedon, and conqueror of the world. I fight not by night, for I scorn to steal victories in the dark, and my men are armed with magic spears of gold and silver and are therefore invincible."

The queen of the Amazons appeared before him, a beautiful woman, with long raven hair. "Greeting to thee, mighty warrior," she said.

"Hast thou come to slay women?"

"Perchance it is you who will triumph over me," replied Alexander.

The queen of the Amazons smiled.

"Then shall it be said of thee," she replied, "that thou wert a valiant warrior who conquered the world, but was himself conquered by women. Is that to be your message to history?"

King Alexander was a man of learning and of wisdom, as well as a great soldier, but the words of the queen of the Amazons were such that he could not answer. He bowed low before the queen and with a gesture indicated that he had naught to say.

"Then it is to be peace," said the queen. "At least, before thy return, let me prepare for thee a banquet."

In a hut made of logs and decorated with skins, a rough wooden table was placed before Alexander and on it was laid a loaf of gold.

"Do ye eat bread of gold?" asked the king, much surprised.

"Nay," replied the queen. "We are women of simple tastes, but thou art a mighty king. If thou didst but wish to eat ordinary bread in this land, why didst thou desire to conquer it? Is there no more bread in your own land that thou shouldst brave the dangers of the dark mountains to eat it here?"

Alexander bowed his head on his breast. Never before had he felt ashamed.

"I, Alexander of Macedon," he said, "was a fool until I came to the land beyond the Mountains of Darkness and learned wisdom from women."

With all haste he returned through the land of eternal night on his Libyan asses. But in the flight the cord was broken. He had to trust entirely to the asses, and many long and weary days and nights did he journey before he saw the light once more.

Alexander found himself in a new and beautiful land. There were no signs of human beings, nor of animals, and a river of the clearest water he had ever seen, flowed gently along. It was full of fish which the soldiers caught quite easily. But a strange thing happened when, after having cut up the fish ready for cooking, they took them to the river to clean them. All the fish came to life again; the pieces joined together and darted away in the water.

At first Alexander would not believe this, but after he had made an experiment himself, he said: "Let all who are wounded bathe in this river, for surely it will cure every ill. This must be the River of Life which flows from Paradise."

He determined to follow the stream to its source and find the Garden of Eden. As he marched along, the valley through which the stream flowed, became narrower and narrower, until, at last, only one person could pass. Alexander continued his journey on foot with a few of his generals walking behind. Mountains, thickly covered with greenest verdure, towered up on either side, the silent river narrowed until it seemed a mere streak of silver flowing gently along, and there was a delicious odor in the air.

At length, where the mountains on either side met, Alexander's path was barred by a great wall of rock. From a tiny fissure the River of Life trickled forth, and beside it was a door of gold, beautifully ornamented. Before this door Alexander paused. Then, drawing his sword, he struck the Gate of Paradise with the hilt.

There was no answer, and Alexander knocked a second time. Again there was no reply, and a third time Alexander knocked with some impatience.

Then the door slowly opened, and a figure in white stood in the entry. In its hand it held a skull, made of gold, with eyes of rubies.

II. THE LAND OF DARKNESS AND THE GATE OF PARADISE | 147

"Who knocks so rudely at the Gate of Paradise?" asked the angel.

"I, Alexander, the Great, of Macedon, the conqueror of the world," answered Alexander, proudly. "I demand admittance to Paradise."

"Hast thou brought peace to the whole world that thou sayest thou art its conqueror?" demanded the angel.

Alexander made no answer.

"Only the righteous who bring peace to man-kind may enter Paradise alive," said the angel, gently.

Alexander hung his head abashed; then, in a voice broken with emotion, he begged that at least he should be given a memento of his visit.

The angel handed him the skull, saying: "Take this and ponder o'er its meaning."

The angel vanished and the golden door closed.

The skull was so heavy that, with all his great strength, Alexander could scarcely carry it. When he placed it in a balance to ascertain its weight, he found that it was heavier than all his treasures. None of his wise men could explain this mystery and so Alexander sought out a Jew among his soldiers, one who had been a student with the rabbis.

Taking a handfull of earth the Jew placed it over the eyes and the skull was then as light as air.

"The meaning is plain," said the Jew. "Not until the human eye is covered with earth--in the grave--is it satisfied. Not until after death can man hope to enter Paradise."

Alexander was anxious to hasten away from that strange region, but many of his soldiers declared that they would settle down by the banks of the River of Life. Next morning, however, the river had vanished. Where all had been beautiful was now only a desolate plain, bounded by bare rocky mountains, reaching to the clouds.

With heavy hearts Alexander's men began their march back.

III--THE WONDERS OF THE WORLD

One day a strange rumbling noise was heard, and toward evening the army halted by the side of a river even more mysterious than the River of Life. It was not a river of water, but of sand and stones. It flowed along with a roaring sound and every few minutes great stones were shot up into the air.

Alexander asked the Jewish soldier if he could explain.

"This," said the Jew, "is the Sambatyon, the river which ceases to flow on the Sabbath."

"And what lies beyond?"

"The land of the Lost Ten Tribes of Israel," was the answer. "None have seen this country."

"Cannot the river then be crossed?" asked Alexander.

"Not by all who wish to cross."

The next day was Friday, and Alexander waited until the evening to see what would happen.

An hour before sunset, at the time of the commencement of Sabbath, the river ceased to flow. The rumbling died down and the Sambatyon appeared like a broad expanse of shining yellow sand.

"To-morrow I shall cross with my army," said Alexander, but next morning the Sambatyon was enveloped in dense black clouds.

Alexander could not see a yard in front of him, and when he ventured on to the sand, the horses sank into it. Flames were also seen in the clouds. After the sun had set and the Sabbath had ended, the clouds cleared away, the rumbling began again and the sand flowed once more like a river.

Alexander was disappointed for a while, but at last he consoled himself with the thought that he had conquered the whole world.

"Now must I carry out my project of ascending above the clouds and afterward descending into the sea," he said, and he proceeded to carry out the instructions given to him in Jerusalem.

Four huge eagles were caught and chained to a big box. At each end of the box was a pole, and on the end of each a brilliant jewel was placed. When all was in readiness, Alexander entered the box and carefully closed the doors.

"Thus did Nimrod ascend into the sky," he said, "but he was a fool. He shot arrows into the air, and when the angels returned them stained with blood, he thought he had killed God. I desire only to see the heavens, not to conquer them."

He gave the signal, and the heads of the eagles chained to the poles were uncovered. The moment they saw the dazzling jewels they tried to snatch them, but could not. So they continued to rise higher and higher until the box was carried above the clouds. By looking through the windows at the top and bottom of the box, Alexander could see how high he was. For a long time he saw nothing but clouds, which appeared like a vast sea beneath him, but when these cleared away, he saw the earth again.

So high was he that the world looked like a ball. Until then he had not known the earth was round. The seas enveloping the greater part of the globe looked like writhing serpents.

"Now I can understand," he said, "why the wise rabbis say that the great fish, the leviathan, surrounds the world with its tail in its mouth."

Then he looked above. The sun seemed further away than ever.

"Heaven is not so near as I thought," he said, and seeing himself but a tiny speck miles above the earth and still further away from the heavens, he grew afraid for the first time in his life. With a stick he knocked the jewels from the poles outside the box, and the eagles, seeing them no longer, began to descend. Alexander breathed more freely when he was safe on the ground again, but he would not tell his generals what he had seen.

"Wait until I have descended into the sea," he said.

Under his orders, a diving bell of clear thick glass, bound with iron, had been constructed. Alexander entered the bell, all the joints were then tightly secured with pitch, and the bell lowered from a ship into the ocean by means of chains.

Before he entered, Alexander took the precaution to put on a magic ring, which his wife, Roxana, had sent him. This, she said, would protect him against the monsters of the deep.

Down, down into the watery deep sank the bell, and for some time Alexander could see nothing. When his eyes grew accustomed to the strange, greenish light, he noticed multitudes of queer fish darting round about the bell. Many were of a shape never conjectured by man, some were so tiny that he could scarcely see them, and others so large that one of these monsters actually tried to swallow the bell. But Alexander showed the magic ring which glowed like a blazing star and the monster darted away.

So deep down sank the bell that no light could at last penetrate from the sun. Most of the fish, however, were luminous, and Alexander was almost dazzled by the changing of the brilliant lights as the denizens of the deep swam swiftly around the bell. Shells of wondrous beauty did he see, together with pearls of great size. The treasures of the deep were revealed to him, and he saw that the riches on land were as nothing compared with them. He saw the coral insects at their work of building, and plants of entrancing beauty growing in the oozy bed of the ocean.

"I wonder," said Alexander, "if I dare venture forth and take some of these beautiful gems back with me. The ring will protect me."

Alexander was one of the bravest men that ever lived, and he immediately set about trying to open the bell. In doing so, he rattled the chains by which it was lowered, and Robus, the officer in charge, took this as a signal to raise the bell.

In his excitement he dropped the chains into the sea, and they fell with a big crash on the bell and smashed it to pieces. When Robus saw what had happened, he cast himself into the sea in a gallant endeavor to rescue his master.

Down below in the glittering depths of the ocean, Alexander saw the fish hurrying away in great fear and he heard the rattling of the chains as they dropped through the water. He looked up and saw them crash on the bell. A terrible, buzzing sound filled his ears, a thousand dazzling colors danced before his eyes and made him giddy.

With great presence of mind he remembered his ring, and immediately a big fish swam underneath him, raised him from the wreckage of the bell and rose swiftly to the surface. Alexander emerged just as Robus dived into the sea. At once he showed the fish his ring and it dived and brought his gallant officer safe to his side.

"I have seen enough," said Alexander, when he was safe on land, "more than mortals should see. I have learned that the earth is for man and that the air above and the waters beneath are for the other and more wonderful creatures of God."

He made preparations to return to Macedon, but his army was wearied with long marching and begged of him to let them rest. Accordingly, he halted outside Babylon. Sickness seized him, but he remembered the warning of the rabbis and would not enter the city. For days he wandered around until his soldiers showed signs of mutiny. Then, throwing caution to the winds, Alexander entered Babylon.

At once his illness took a serious turn, and in a few days he died. When the Jews heard the news, they mourned him sincerely, for they knew that they had lost a good friend. All that re-mains as a memorial of Alexander is the city of Alexandria, which he founded in Egypt. It stands to this day.

Copyright © 2019 / Alicia Éditions
Credits: Canva, Sol Aronson
All rights reserved

www.ingramcontent.com/pod-product-compliance
Lightning Source LLC
LaVergne TN
LVHW092010090526
838202LV00002B/81